The Case of
the Mystery Graves

The Case of
the Mystery Graves

GORDON SNELL

POOLBEG

Published 1998 by
Poolbeg Press Ltd,
123 Baldoyle Industrial Estate,
Dublin 13, Ireland

© Gordon Snell 1998

The moral right of the author has been asserted.

The Arts Council
An Chomhairle Ealaíon

A catalogue record for this book is available from the British Library.

ISBN 1 85371 898 X

Cover illustration by Peter Hanan
Cover design by Poolbeg Group Services Ltd
Set by Poolbeg Group Services Ltd in Stone Serif 9.5/14.5
Printed and bound in Great Britain by
Cox & Wyman Ltd, Reading, Berkshire.

About the Author

Gordon Snell is a well-known scriptwriter and author of books for children and adults. Other books in this series include *Dangerous Treasure*, *The Mystery of Monk Island*, *The Curse of Werewolf Castle* and *The Phantom Horseman*. He is also the author of *The Tex & Sheelagh Omnibus*. He lives in Dalkey, Co Dublin, and is married to the writer Maeve Binchy.

Other books in the series

Dangerous Treasure
The Mystery of Monk Island
The Curse of Werewolf Castle
The Phantom Horseman

Published by Poolbeg

For dearest Maeve, with all my love

Contents

CHAPTER ONE

The Pirate's Grave

"Hey, Dessy, look at this! A letter from Hollywood!" Brendan waved the bright yellow envelope in the air as he and his cousin Molly walked across the small park near Brendan's house. Dessy stopped practising his football dribbling and came to meet them.

"Yep, I was expecting an offer, all right," he said. "Gabriel Byrne was going for the part too, but I guess they liked me better."

"Do you want to know what's in it, or not?" asked Molly.

"Bet you never saw a letter like this," said Brendan, taking a sheet of paper out. It was bright yellow, like the envelope, and when he opened it out, there was a full-colour picture at the top of the page, with little stars all round it, and underneath in big red letters the words BILLY BANTAM.

"He was always a modest fella, our Billy!" Dessy exclaimed.

"Is he coming to make another movie here?" Billy Bantam was the child star they had met when the horror movie *The Curse of Werewolf Castle* was being filmed around Molly's home at Ballygandon. They had thought him vain and stuck-up at first, but when strange things started to happen on the movie set and Billy was threatened, they had come to his rescue. Since then they had been good friends.

Brendan read from the letter: "Hi there, folks! How do you like my new writing-paper? The studio got it for me, to reply to my fans. Isn't it a laugh?"

"I'm glad he doesn't take it seriously," said Dessy.

"I'm sure you wouldn't mind having your ugly face on a letter," said Molly.

"Only for the sake of my fans," said Dessy. "Anyway, what does he say?"

"He says some friends of his called Grace and Brad are coming to Ireland with their parents, and he'd like us to meet them. They've been told their ancestors came from somewhere around Molly's part of the country."

"It's odd, though," said Molly. "Their surname is Darly, and I've never heard of anyone of that name in our area."

"Maybe they hated it so much, the whole bunch of them emigrated at once!" Dessy grinned.

"You're a scream, Dessy," said Molly. "I was going to ask if you and Brendan would like to come

2

and stay next weekend, and we could investigate the graveyard at Lisbeg where their family is meant to be. But now you can just stay put here, and Brendan can come on his own."

"Oh, go on, let him come," said Brendan. "He's sorry, aren't you, Dessy?"

"Of course," said Dessy, "I was just joking. What else does Billy say?"

"He says there's a firm in Hollywood called Tree Tracers who have partners in Ireland, and they made this discovery about the Darly family tree. And he also says at the end: *Don't forget you are invited any time to visit with us. You could watch me working on a new movie.*"

"I wish we could go," said Molly.

"And *I* wish I could fly to the moon," said Dessy. "There's about as much chance of doing that as affording the fare to California."

"Billy said he'd pay part of the fare for us," said Brendan.

"And where will we get the rest?" asked Dessy. "Even if we found some cheap fares, we'd still have to win the Lottery to afford them."

"We'll have to start finding jobs to do," said Brendan. "Washing cars and such."

"Even if we had the money," said Molly gloomily, "our parents wouldn't let us go on our own."

"Listen, I've got an idea," said Brendan. "You know Mrs Boyd who runs Horseshoe House, where Grandpa Locky lives now? She said she would be

3

visiting America some time, and she could take us over to see Billy."

"Let's go and see her at the weekend," Molly said. "I'd like to go and see Grandpa anyway."

"Yeah," said Dessy in a fake American accent, "we can tell her 'Say, sister, the boys and I are making you an offer you can't refuse. You're gonna take us to the US of A'!"

"Oh, I'm quite sure she'd be persuaded by that," said Brendan.

"OK, let's give it a try," said Molly. "On one condition."

"What's that?" asked Dessy.

"That you keep your mouth shut," Molly answered.

They caught the bus from Ballygandon to visit Horseshoe House, and Brendan and Molly's grandfather Locky met them as they walked up the leafy drive.

"It's good to see you all!" he said. "I haven't seen *you* for a while, Dessy. As I recall, you were going to start on a career as a stand-up comic."

"Sure," said Dessy. "What did the computer have for its tea?"

"I don't know," said Locky.

"Fish and micro-chips!"

"Not bad," said Locky. "You could have your own series before long."

"Let's hope so," said Dessy. "I need the money."

"We all do," said Brendan. He explained about the invitation to Hollywood from Billy Bantam, and the problem of finding the fare.

"If I had the money, I'd give it to you," said Locky. "Unfortunately my horses haven't been running as fast as they should. In fact I think some of them are still looking for the winning-post."

Even though finding the fare was still a problem, they were in luck with Mrs Boyd. She said she was planning to go to see her daughter in California at the end of June, and she would be happy for them to travel there and back with her.

"That leaves us just over eight weeks to get the money for the fare," said Molly.

They decided to make a list of the jobs they could do to make a bit of money. Car-washing, newspaper rounds, lawn-mowing, window-cleaning, baby-sitting . . .

"And maybe you could work in a pub," said Locky. "I did that for a while as a young fella. I can pull a great pint still, I dare say. I'd show you how."

"Grandpa, you don't seriously think they'd give kids like us a job in a pub?" asked Brendan in amazement.

"I suppose not," said Locky. "I'd forgotten you were so young. Or maybe I'd forgotten I was so old."

"What about grave-digging?" said Dessy suddenly. "Do you think that pays well?"

"What a gruesome idea," said Molly.

"What made you think of that?" asked Locky.

"I remembered those friends of Billy's coming over to look at that graveyard," said Dessy.

"Which one?" asked Locky.

"Lisbeg, not far from Ballygandon," said Molly. "We were going to go and take a look at it."

"That's where Sailor Jack is buried," said Locky. "A real rogue, he was. They say he haunts the place."

"Tell us about him, Grandpa," said Brendan eagerly. Locky had some fantastic tale to tell about almost any place you could mention.

"We'll go and take a look," said Locky, "and I can tell you the story on the way."

As they bumped along the winding country roads in Locky's ancient car, he told them the story of Sailor Jack.

"He was an adventurer in the last century," said Locky. "He came from the Ballygandon area, and went to sea as a young lad. He was smart and quite ruthless too, and determined to make a fortune for himself. He got to be leader of a gang of pirates who terrorised the seas from the North Atlantic down to the Caribbean."

"And did he make a fortune?" asked Dessy.

"So they say," said Locky. "He certainly came home and lived in fine style, but he was a mean so-and-so, and wouldn't give a penny to help anyone, even when there was the famine and people were starving."

6

"What happened to him in the end?" asked Brendan.

"He was murdered by one of his old shipmates who came to him asking for money. Sailor Jack just laughed at him, and the man got so angry he picked up an axe and felled him to the ground."

"So what happened to his money?" Molly wondered.

"Well," said Locky, "the story goes that Sailor Jack had it hidden somewhere. He had prepared a grave for himself in that very graveyard of Lisbeg, and people believed he kept the gold hidden there. But other people say the inscription on the tombstone has some kind of code which says where the treasure is. No one knows the real truth."

"And no one's found the treasure?" Dessy asked.

"Never," said Locky. "But of course they've tried. You'll see the results when we get to Lisbeg."

They found the graveyard beside a remote country road. It was a mile away from the old village of Lisbeg, which was now ruined and deserted. At the entrance to the graveyard there was a broken-down stone gateway with a rusty iron gate that hung off one remaining hinge. There were trees all around the sides of the graveyard, growing beside the tumbledown wall that surrounded it.

The tombstones stuck up from the long, rough grass, some leaning at odd angles. The place was neglected and overgrown with long grass and brambles, and had a gloomy, eerie feeling about it, even in daylight. Brendan thought that it must be a really scary place at night, especially if Sailor Jack's ghost was on the prowl.

"Sailor Jack's tomb is over there in the far corner, I think," said Locky. They wound their way between the gravestones, many of them covered in moss and ivy so that it was hard to read the inscriptions.

They came to a tall tombstone with a carving on top which looked like a skull.

"The skull and crossbones," said Locky. "Old Sailor Jack didn't mind who knew about his pirate days. In fact he boasted about them."

"Someone's made a bit of a mess of his grave, haven't they?" said Dessy. They stood looking down at the stones scattered around near the tall tombstone. There was a hollow in the ground which other stones had fallen into.

Locky said, "People didn't mind what kind of a mess they made, if they could only find the treasure. No wonder he haunts the place. And I wouldn't be surprised if he's laughing at the robbers he's foiled."

Brendan looked closely at the tombstone. It was dusty and dirty, but he could just make out the letters of the inscription. Brendan read it aloud:

"Here lie the mortal remains of JACK MORAN, king of the high seas.

I was born on the 7th day of the 1st month of the year 1829, at 5 o'clock in the morning.

My spirit will never die. Beware all who meddle with this noble grave. Torment shall be theirs. Rest in peace, Jack, as your enemies never will."

"That's a weird kind of an epitaph," said Molly.

"He was a weird kind of a bloke," said Locky.

"Maybe that inscription has the clue to where he hid his treasure," said Brendan. "I'll write it down. Maybe we can crack the code." He started copying the words into a small notebook.

"Somebody may have cracked it already," said Molly. "Who's to know if the treasure might have been found and spent long ago?"

"It could have been, but I don't think so," said Locky. "You see, the stories all say that anyone who dug in this grave looking for the treasure, came to a bad end. One man went mad and threw himself off a cliff. Another was found wandering around the graveyard, moaning and screaming, and pointing at something horrible he seemed to think was coming after him. Sailor Jack's Revenge, the local people called it."

"Well, one thing's for sure," said Dessy, "I'm not going near that grave." He raised his hand to his mouth and called, "Do you hear me, Sailor Jack? You're safe from Dessy!"

The others smiled nervously. Brendan looked around the deserted graveyard. He was puzzled. There seemed almost to be a presence there, something else besides their small group around the tomb. And it must have been the wind in the trees he was hearing, but there was a sound that was very like a faint, sneering laugh . . .

9

CHAPTER TWO

Suspicions

Molly, Brendan and Dessy were sitting on the wall of the yard outside Molly's parents' shop, waiting for the Darly family to arrive. It was a Saturday, just over two weeks since they had got Billy Bantam's letter about the Darlys.

"They may be a real pain," said Dessy. "California people always think their state is the bee's knees, and everywhere else is rubbish."

"Well, Billy's from California, and we got to like him, didn't we?" said Molly.

"Yes, but we don't know anything about these Darlys. Grace and Brad," Dessy pronounced the names in a fake American drawl. "What kind of a name is Brad, for heaven's sake?"

"It's a good film star's name," said Brendan. "Look at Brad Pitt. In fact, when the talent scouts find me in Hollywood, I think I might use it as my screen name. BRAD O'HARA. It would look good in lights."

"We've got to find the fare to Hollywood first," said Molly.

In the past two weeks they had all been doing their best to find money-making jobs to do at weekends and before and after school. Dessy had been taking bottles to the bottle bank for some neighbours who consumed more bottles than they cared to admit. Brendan had been doing a newspaper round, and taking his aunt Lily's yappy little dog out for walks. But he lost that job after the dog slipped his lead and started to chase a cat which turned around and spat and then ended up chasing the dog.

Molly had earned some pocket money helping her father and mother stack shelves in their grocery shop, and she had also been baby-sitting for friends in Ballygandon who had a toddler called Alison. She behaved like an angel all the time until her parents came home, then she started whingeing and crying. So Molly's reputation as a baby-sitter was ruined. It was very unfair.

All these activities had helped the Hollywood fund, but they still had a very long way to go. At least their parents had agreed that they could travel with Mrs Boyd, if they could find the money for the fare.

"What about forgery?" said Dessy with a grin. "Brendan could photograph a twenty-pound note and then make lots of copies."

"I'm sure it's been tried," said Brendan, "and the people who tried it are serving jail sentences right now."

"That reminds me," said Dessy, "what did the bank robber's belt say to his trousers?"

"I don't know, Dessy," said Molly.

"This is a hold-up!"

"You should be in jail yourself," said Brendan, "for making jokes like that."

Just then they saw a green car coming slowly along the road towards them. As it neared them, they could see the driver peering around her, and the man in the passenger seat pointing at a map he held in front of him. There were two children in the back seat.

"I'm sure this must be the Darlys," said Molly. She waved, and the car drew up beside them.

The man leaned out of the window and said, "Pardon me, miss, can you direct us to the Donovans' house?"

"This is it," said Molly, jumping down off the wall. "You must be the Darlys."

"We sure are," said the man. "Paul Darly, that's me. How do you do?" He leaned out of the window and shook hands, saying, "I guess you must be Molly?"

"That's right," said Molly, "and this is my cousin Brendan and our friend Dessy."

"Oh, we've heard a lot about you from Billy and his mother," said Paul Darly. "I'm delighted to meet you all." He leaned into the car and said, "Susan, meet the Donovans."

"I'd better park the car first," said Susan Darly.

"This way," said Molly, waving the car in at the

gate and into the yard. Susan Darly got out and shook hands, just as Molly's mother came out of the shop. Grace and Brad got out of the back of the car. They both had ginger-coloured hair and freckles, and wore jeans and tee-shirts. Grace's had a flower design on it, and Brad's said DODGERS.

They all went inside for some tea and soft drinks, and then Molly's mother said, "Molly, why don't you three show Grace and Brad around the village, while we have a chat with Paul and Susan?"

"That would be great," said Brad.

"There's not much to see around here, to be honest," said Dessy. "You'll have to come to Dublin to see the real sights."

"Dessy's just a Dublin jackeen," said Molly, "he doesn't understand that the country is the real Ireland. Besides, we've got lots of things in Ballygandon, fishing and swimming and horse-riding, and even a haunted castle."

"Well, I think your country is just great," said Grace. "I wish we lived in a beautiful place like this."

"But Los Angeles must be fantastic," said Brendan.

"I guess so, in some ways," said Brad, "but you can get awful tired of cars and freeways."

"Ballygandon's the right kind of size, I reckon," said Grace.

Molly smiled with pride, and said to Dessy and Brendan, "There, you see! At last we've met some people with a bit of good taste."

They wandered round the village and along the

river, and then climbed the hill up to the ruined castle. They told Brad and Grace some of the legends of feuds and murders here in the ancient times, and how more recently *The Curse of Werewolf Castle* had been filmed here.

"We saw that movie," said Grace, "it was one of Billy's. Real horror stuff."

"We were in it too, as a matter of fact," said Brendan casually. "We were peasant children."

"And I played this," said Molly, producing her tin whistle and sounding a few notes.

"Yes, I remember," said Grace. Molly thought it was good of her to *say* she remembered, even if she was only being polite.

"I love Irish music," said Brad. "Maybe you could teach us Irish dancing. We'd wow them back home."

"We'll have a go," said Molly.

"Personally I'm more into rock and roll," said Dessy.

"Right now I guess we'd better get back," said Grace. "Mom and Dad are planning to meet the Tree Tracer man this afternoon and see if they can find the grave of Dad's ancestor."

"We met his partner in Tree Tracers, Doctor Galvin, in LA," said Brad. "She's a specialist in family trees and all that stuff. Dad is really into all this ancestor-tracing, finding his roots and so on. I'm more interested in here and now than the past, but he seems to think it's worth the money to find out where the family came from."

As they walked down the hill and back to the Donovans' store, they told Brad and Grace about their visit to Lisbeg, and the story of Sailor Jack and his haunting.

"Boy, you certainly had violent times around here in the past," said Brad.

"In LA we have violent times in the *present*," said Grace.

"We can cope with that," said Dessy, who saw himself caught up perhaps in a hundred-mile-an-hour car chase after gangsters, or foiling a hold-up in a liquor store. "It ain't no problem to the Ballygandon Private Eyes."

Brad smiled. "OK, Dessy, how about this deal? You teach us Irish dancing, and we'll teach you how to talk in a *real* American accent?"

Molly and Brendan laughed. Dessy just grunted.

Molly's parents told the Darlys they must come and have tea with them next day, since they were staying in the nearby town.

"Thanks for a great welcome," said Paul Darly. "Now, Susan, are you sure you know the way over to Lisbeg?"

"Haven't the Donovans just drawn it for us on the map," said his wife, "and won't you be navigating?"

"We'll ride our bikes over there and meet you when you've found the grave," said Molly.

"Great, see you there then," said Grace.

An hour later when they reached Lisbeg, Molly,

Brendan and Dessy parked their bikes near the old stone gateway of the graveyard. They looked over the wall. In the far corner, the other side of the graveyard from Sailor Jack's grave, they saw the Darlys grouped around a tombstone. They were taking photographs of it, and of each other. They were clearly pleased to have found the grave of one of their family.

"Let's go over and have a look at it," said Dessy. "Maybe the Darlys buried treasure in their grave, like Sailor Jack."

They were about to go through the gate when Molly held up her hand to stop them. "Wait a minute," she said quietly.

"What's up?" asked Brendan.

"You see that man with them?" said Molly.

"Yes," said Brendan, "I suppose he's the Tree Tracer fellow who found the grave for them."

"Don't you recognise him?" said Molly.

"He looks familiar all right," said Dessy.

"That's Séamus Gallagher, who runs the pub over in Killbreen," said Molly. "I'd know that bald head and that fierce expression anywhere."

They had all come across Séamus Gallagher during the filming of *The Curse of Werewolf Castle*. He thought the movie should have been made in Killbreen instead of Ballygandon, and there was a strong suspicion that he had set fire to the scenery one night out of spite. What was he doing here, helping Americans to trace their ancestry? Molly suspected that he knew as little about family trees as the Man in the Moon.

"What's he doing here?" asked Dessy.

"I don't know," said Molly, "but whatever it is, you can bet he's up to no good."

"The Darlys seem delighted with him, anyway," said Brendan. "Look, they're shaking him by the hand."

"And giving him some cash too," said Molly, as they watched Paul Darly take out his wallet and hand over several notes to Séamus Gallagher. They saw Séamus smiling and nodding with delight as he pocketed the money. Then he began to walk back towards the gate.

"He mustn't see us," said Brendan. "Hide the bikes!" They pushed their bicycles into some bushes that grew not far from the gate, then crept along the wall to the corner and went round it. They crouched down, peering round the corner. They saw Séamus Gallagher come out of the gate, whistling and patting his pocket.

Then he turned and waved at the Darlys, who were still down at the far end of the graveyard, looking at the grave and taking more photographs. Séamus walked away from them down the road to where they saw he had parked his Land-Rover. He got into it and drove away. The three came out of their hiding-place and retrieved their bikes from the bushes.

"I think it would be best if we didn't tell the Darlys we know Séamus," said Molly. "They seem so delighted with whatever he's shown them."

17

"Besides, we don't know for certain that he's done anything crooked," said Brendan.

"If he has, we'll find out," said Molly. "The Ballygandon Gang never fails."

They threaded their way between the tombstones, across the tangled grass.

"Hi there!" said Paul Darly. "Well, we found what we were looking for. A genuine Darly grave. Imagine, this is where they buried my great-great-great-grandfather. See, it says: *Here lies Gerard Darly, 1810 to 1872.* And then underneath: *And his beloved wife Patricia, 1819 to 1876.* I guess it was their son Donal who emigrated and founded the Darly dynasty in the States. Mr Gallagher and his Tree Tracers will do a full family tree for us."

They all went back across the graveyard and the Darlys said goodbye. They were going to come back the next day and tidy up the grave. They would call on the Donovans in the afternoon.

When the three had waved to the Darlys in the departing car, Molly said, "I want to go back and have a closer look at that tombstone. I'm sure there's something fishy about all this."

They made their way back across the graveyard. Molly knelt down and examined the lettering of the inscription. "There's something odd here," she said.

They all leaned over and peered at the epitaph.

Brendan ran his fingers over the carved letters. "Yes," he said firmly, "someone has definitely been tampering with this tombstone!"

CHAPTER THREE

Mrs Trout and Mr Salmon

"See where it says: *Here lies Gerard Darly*," said Brendan. "The letters in *Darly* look sort of squashed together."

Molly began to scrape at the carved-out letters with her fingernail. There was an ancient crust of dirt in each, which had got ingrained in the stone over the years. But when she came to the letter *r*, the dirt came away easily, and they could see bright, clean stone.

"It's just as if that one letter had only been chiselled out recently," she said.

"You've got it!" said Brendan. "That's the answer. I thought the letters looked squashed up. It could be because someone has added the *r* in the middle."

"Yes, that's right," said Molly. "The inscription originally said: *Here lies Gerard Daly*. Add an *r* and you've got a grave to show the *Darly* family."

"No prizes for guessing who added the letter," said Dessy.

"Séamus Gallagher," said Molly and Brendan together.

"He must have found out the Darlys were looking for their roots, and faked a tombstone to show them," said Brendan.

"And charged them a lot of money for doing it," said Dessy, "judging by the cash they were handing over to him."

"But how would he know about the Darlys in the first place?" Brendan wondered.

"Remember that Doctor something-or-other that Brad and Grace said they met in LA?" said Molly. "She was a partner in the Tree Tracer firm, they said."

"So maybe she told Séamus about the Darlys, and he found a suitable grave he could fix up," said Brendan.

"It's a neat trick, when you come to think of it," said Dessy. "Look what we could do with *your* name. Brendan O'Hara could easily be changed to Brendan O'Horror! The possibilities are endless."

"Seriously, Dessy," said Molly, "the possibilities *are* endless. Séamus and his Doctor pal could be doing this all the time. There's plenty of tombstones with all sorts of names here, not to mention all the other graveyards around."

"You mean tricking the Darlys is not just a one-off fraud by a couple of chancers?" said Brendan. "They're running it as a regular operation?"

"They must be," said Molly. "The Darlys

wouldn't have fallen for it if it hadn't looked quite professional. This LA person probably has a slick office and brochures and stuff."

"You can bet she is more likely to be the brains of the outfit than Séamus, anyway," said Brendan.

"Yes," Molly agreed, "he'd just do the dirty work at this end. He'd be well able for that."

"We need to find out what kind of a deal they offer," said Brendan. "If we're going to expose Séamus Gallagher, we need all the evidence we can get."

"We'll start by doing our own tracing," said Molly, "and track down Tree Tracers!"

When they got back to Molly's house, they gathered in her room. Molly had brought the telephone directory upstairs and they spread it on the floor and sat around it.

Brendan leafed through the T's and looked disappointed. "There's nothing listed under TREE."

"Those are personal names in the front bit," said Molly. "We should look at the yellow pages in the second half. That's where the firms and businesses are."

She turned to the yellow pages and found TREE there. "There's quite a few of them," she said, and read out: *"Barker Tree Service. Tree Felling, Wood Chipper, Stump Grinding . . . "*

"Yuk," said Dessy, "that sounds like the dentist."

"Yes, there's *Tree Surgeons* too," said Molly, "if you fancy an operation on your head."

"I can't see anything about tree tracing or family trees," said Brendan.

"We're looking at the wrong kind of trees," said Molly. "It must be under something else. What's that word for the research they do into family history and such?"

"Yes, I know," said Dessy. "Gynaecology!"

"That means having babies, you eejit," said Molly.

"But it's something like that," said Brendan. "Yes, I've got it. Genealogy!"

"I wasn't far wrong," said Dessy.

Molly turned the pages, and said excitedly, "Here it is! GENEALOGICAL RESEARCH. Then it lists several names. *Family Origins Agency, Genealogy and Nomenclature Institute . . .*"

"They certainly go in for long words in this game," said Dessy.

"Here it is," cried Molly. "*Tree Tracers, specialists in heritage research*. Then it gives a telephone number. And guess where it is? Killbreen!"

"What a coincidence!" Brendan laughed. "That's where Séamus Gallagher lives."

"I'm just going to check something," said Molly, turning the pages to the P section. "Now, here we are: *Public Houses and Lounge Bars*, it says; there's certainly a huge list of *them*! And there's Séamus's place, *Gallagher's Bar, Killbreen*. And it's the same number as *Tree Tracers*."

"Well, whatever set-up they have in LA," said Brendan, "they can't have much of an office here."

"Let's ring him up," said Dessy, "and tell him his cover's blown and we're coming after him."

"Not so fast, Dessy," said Molly. "We've got to collect the evidence, so we have a watertight case. I suggest we ring him, yes, but pretend we're people looking for family trees and ancestors, and want to know about his service."

They went downstairs. The living-room was empty. Molly's parents were both busy in the shop. Molly closed the door and went across to where the telephone stood on a table beside the window.

She dialled the number, and held the receiver slightly away from her ear. Brendan and Dessy put their heads close, so that they too could hear what was said.

"Hello, Gallagher's," said Séamus's gruff voice at the other end.

"Oh, gee whiz," said Molly, putting on what she thought was a southern-states American drawl. "I must have the wrong number. I was hoping to find Tree Tracers."

"Yes, this is Tree Tracers," said Séamus, trying to sound posh. "Can I help you, ma'am?"

"You-all sure can," said Molly, warming to the part, while Brendan and Dessy held their hands over their mouths to stop themselves laughing. "My name is Mrs Trout, and I'm hoping you-all can help me find my Irish ancestors."

"Well, certainly, I'm sure we can," said Séamus in a smarmy voice. "Give me your address and telephone number, and I'll have our LA office call you with full details."

"Well, as I'm here in your area," said Molly, "I was hoping to call in to your office here. I can come over to Killbreen and meet you at your headquarters there."

Séamus began to bluster. The last thing he wanted was for a rich client to discover that the fancy firm of Tree Tracers operated out of a dingy pub. "That wouldn't really be . . . it wouldn't be convenient just now. We have the builders in, we're expanding . . . putting in extra computers and so on. Why don't we meet, say, at Killbreen Bridge? It's a nice spot, very historic. Then I can give you all the details."

"Fine, just fine," said Molly.

"Shall we say eleven o'clock tomorrow morning?" said Séamus.

"Fine," said Molly, without thinking. "Goodbye now!" She put the phone down.

"What are we going to do now?" asked Dessy. "You had him fooled on the phone, Molly; in fact, your American accent was almost as good as mine, but I don't think you could make even a dunderhead like Séamus believe you're an all-American lady."

"It's a problem all right," said Molly. "I got carried away."

"Who can we get to pretend to be Mrs Trout?" Brendan wondered. "Why did you choose that name, by the way?"

"I like fishing for trout," said Molly, "*and* eating them."

"There's no one we can ask," said Brendan. "Séamus knows all your family, and he knows the Darlys too."

"He doesn't know Locky!" said Molly.

"Your grandfather?" Dessy burst out laughing. "Are you going to dress him up in drag and bring him flouncing along to meet Séamus? This I've got to see."

"We'll get him to say Mrs Trout is sick, and he's a friend who's come instead," said Molly.

"Will he do it?" asked Brendan.

"I'm pretty sure he will," said Molly. "Locky's game for any kind of adventure."

She was right. When they rang their grandfather, he was delighted with the idea. He even suggested he should wear a cowboy hat and pretend to be a Texan.

"I think it's better if you just behave ordinarily, Grandpa," said Molly. "You don't even have to put on an accent. You can say you emigrated to America when you were grown up."

"I sometimes wonder if he ever did grow up," whispered Brendan.

Molly smiled and said down the phone, "Thanks, Grandpa, we'll meet you just outside Killbreen on the Ballygandon road, about half past ten tomorrow."

They saw Grandpa Locky's old car bumping along the road towards them, and waved. He pulled up beside them and said, "Hello there! I see the Fraud Squad's Private Eyes have come out in full force. OK, let's go get him."

"We're not arresting him, Grandpa," said Molly.

"Pity," said Locky, "I was practising my lines. *Anything you say may be taken down and used in evidence . . .*"

"We just want you to find out how their scam works," Brendan explained. "What they charge, and how they operate, and who the partner in LA is."

"So when we're over there in California we can track down the fraudster at that end," said Dessy. "Then we can call in the cops."

"Let's concentrate on Killbreen for the moment," said Molly. "Grandpa, if you take us to the bridge now, we can hide underneath it, on the river-bank. There's a footpath there. Then we can hear what you and Séamus Gallagher say."

"Good thinking, detective," said Locky. "Let's go."

They crouched down under the stone arch of the bridge that spanned the river. Locky was waiting on the bridge above. They saw his face as he leaned over and said, "There's a fellow coming this way, a bald grumpy-looking character."

Molly nodded and gave him the thumbs-up sign. In a few moments they heard Locky say, "Pardon me, sir, but would you be from Tree Tracers?"

"I am indeed," said Séamus Gallagher. They

heard Locky explain that he was a friend of Mrs Trout, who was sorry not to be able to come herself because she wasn't well.

"I think it was the fish she ate last night," said Locky.

"Too bad," said Séamus. "Are you from the Trout family yourself?"

"No, I'm just a friend," said Locky. "My name is Salmon. Rock Salmon."

Dessy giggled. But Brendan muttered, "If he goes on like that, Séamus will realise he's faking."

"You mean Mr Salmon is only *codding*?" grinned Dessy.

"Sssh, listen!" whispered Molly.

They heard Séamus tell Locky that he was sure the name Trout definitely had Irish origins, and with the help of their LA office and their computerised bank of historical data, they would surely be able to find a family grave.

"I wouldn't be surprised if it turned out to be quite local," said Séamus. "Somewhere around here, in fact."

"I wouldn't be at *all* surprised, either," whispered Molly.

"What Mrs Trout was wondering," they heard Locky say, "was how much it might cost to do the tracing. Between you and me, she's not short of a bob or two, so she wouldn't be trying to do it on the cheap."

"Well now," said Séamus, sounding very pleased,

"I don't think you'll find our charges excessive, considering the service we provide. I have a brochure here which will explain it all. And of course, if there was a cash payment, we could let you have a small reduction."

"That's very generous," said Locky. "Well, if you can begin your researches, I'm sure Mrs Trout will get in touch with you soon and firm up the deal, as it were."

Locky and Séamus said goodbye and Locky went back to his car which was parked near the bridge. After a while they heard him say, "OK, you can come out now."

The three of them scrambled up the bank and on to the road, and got into Locky's car. He showed them the brochure Séamus had given him.

"Wow!" said Molly as they looked at it. "They certainly know how to charge. Look at this. Five hundred pounds for locating a grave, another hundred for photographs, two hundred for a scroll showing the family tree. They must be making a fortune."

"And what's the betting," said Dessy, "that Séamus will be out in Lisbeg graveyard as soon as possible, looking for a name that he can change to TROUT?"

"I'm sure he will be," said Brendan, "probably this very afternoon. And I think the Ballygandon Gang should mount a surveillance operation to watch him."

CHAPTER FOUR

Laughter from the Grave

When they arrived at Lisbeg, the graveyard was deserted. The grey, cloudy sky seemed to hang heavily over the tombstones, which stood there, Brendan thought, like a crowd that had gathered for some event and then been turned to stone. Even though the day was quite warm, there seemed to be a chill about the place, and it was easy to think that the sighing of the wind in the trees was something more – the murmur of ghostly presences hovering among the graves.

"Brendan, we're talking to you!" Molly's voice broke into his daydream.

He blinked and said, "Sorry, I was just thinking."

"That makes a change," said Dessy.

"We've got a plan," said Molly. "Dessy's going to keep watch at the gate to see when Séamus is coming. You and I will check out the graves, to see if we can work out which one he might choose."

"OK," said Brendan. "We'd better hide our bikes first."

They put the bicycles in the bushes, and Dessy sat down by the gate-post, looking up the road. Brendan and Molly threaded their way between the tombstones.

Brendan pointed to the far corner and said, "Look, the Darlys have tidied up the family grave."

They went over to it. The stones that formed a rectangle round the grave had been lined up neatly, and the grass that grew on the mound in the centre had been trimmed. There was a vase of fresh flowers on the grave too.

After yesterday's discovery, Molly had put back the dirt she had scraped away from the new letter *r* on the tombstone, so that the Darlys wouldn't realise what Séamus had been up to. For the present anyway, it was kinder to let them think they had found the right grave. And they didn't want to blow the whistle on Séamus until they had found out the full extent of the dodgy business he was mixed up in. Molly felt they would only find that out if they could make their investigations at the Los Angeles end. She had to keep hoping they'd be able to make the trip.

"Come on," said Brendan, "let's look at some of the other names."

They wandered among the tombstones, reading out the names.

"*O'Driscoll* . . ." said Brendan. "Then here's a *McKenna* . . . and a *Flynn* . . . I can't see anything remotely like *Trout*. You may have set Séamus quite a problem there."

"Hey, look at this!" said Molly.

Brendan came over to her. *"In loving memory of Paul German,"* he read.

"German is what it says now," said Molly. "But look at the *e*. It's been messed about with. I'm sure it was originally an *o*, and the name was *Gorman*. That's a common name around here."

"Séamus must have been sent a family called German by his LA partner," said Brendan. "The sooner we can get over there and check her out, the better."

"Do you really think we'll get there?" asked Molly.

"I'm sure of it," said Brendan, "I just have this hunch. I'm certain when the summer holidays come round, we'll be off."

Their wanderings through the graveyard had brought them to the grave of Sailor Jack. They looked at the tumbled stones and the tombstone with its boastful, threatening inscription.

"I wonder if he does rest in peace," said Molly.

"I doubt it," said Brendan. "He probably hovers around here, making sure no one messes with his grave."

"He hasn't been very successful by the look of it," said Molly.

"Maybe," said Brendan, "but remember what happened to the people who tried it."

31

"I wonder if there *is* a code in that inscription," said Molly.

"And I wonder if anyone has cracked it," said Brendan. "Perhaps we could be the first. I've been trying to puzzle out what it could be."

Just then they heard a high-pitched whistle from up by the gate. It was Dessy's signal that Séamus Gallagher was on the way. They looked across and saw Dessy pointing down the road. Then he disappeared behind the wall.

"Where's he gone?" said Brendan.

"He's probably hiding in the bushes up by the gate," said Molly.

"And where are *we* going to hide?" Brendan said anxiously. "We can't get back to the gate in time, he'll arrive and see us."

"We'll have to stay here," said Molly. "Come on." She scrambled over the stone boundary wall of the graveyard, which was just behind Sailor Jack's grave. There were thick bushes there and they could hide among those and still see over the wall into the graveyard. Brendan joined her.

In the gap between the distant gate-posts, they saw Séamus Gallagher's Land-Rover pull up. Séamus got out and they heard him say, "Stay, boy, stay!" They heard a bark.

"He's brought that horrible dog with him," said Brendan.

"Yes, Lonnigan," said Molly. "Remember how they tried to get him to play a werewolf in the horror movie, and he messed up the whole thing?"

"He got booted off the film, and Séamus with him," Brendan laughed.

"It's just as well he's leaving him in the Land-Rover," said Molly. "If Séamus brought him down here, he might sniff us out."

They watched Séamus enter the graveyard, and look around. He consulted a notebook, flicking through the pages.

"What do you think that is?" asked Brendan.

"Maybe a list of the names on the tombstones," said Molly. "He's trying to match one up with *Trout*."

"It's a fishy business all right," grinned Brendan.

"Your jokes are getting as bad as Dessy's," said Molly.

"Look, there *is* Dessy!" Brendan pointed to the far side of the graveyard. They could see Dessy's head peering over the wall, near the gate. He was no doubt wondering where they were hiding. Séamus looked up from his notebook, and Dessy ducked down.

Séamus began to walk among the graves, looking at the names. Then he noticed the Darly grave, and went across to it. They could see him staring down at it, and noticing the clearing-up that the Darlys had done. They saw him chuckling to himself.

Then he looked at his notebook, and began to roam about again, peering at the tombstones. He stopped beside one, and bent down and examined the inscription. He ran his fingers along it, then stood back and smiled. He made a note in his book.

"It looks as if he's found a name to change," whispered Brendan.

"I expect he'll be back with his hammer and chisel, and then he'll be ready to show Mrs Trout the family's tomb," said Molly.

"And collect the money," Brendan nodded.

They watched Séamus put the notebook in his pocket. Then he turned and looked in the direction of Sailor Jack's grave, and Molly and Brendan's hiding-place. He began to walk towards them.

"He's coming this way!" said Molly in alarm. They crouched in the bushes and watched as Séamus came striding across towards Sailor Jack's grave. He stopped in front of it, and gazed at the tombstone.

"Jack Moran!" he said gruffly. "You crafty old pirate. 'King of the High Seas' indeed! I'll find your treasure, one of these days." He suddenly leaned forward and gripped the tombstone in both hands, staring at the inscription. He looked as if he would like to tear it out of the ground. "I'll find it, do you hear me?" he growled.

Brendan could not resist the temptation. In a faint, wailing voice he said, "I . . . hear . . . you . . . "

They saw Séamus Gallagher let go of the tombstone and leap backwards. He stood there shaking, and staring in terror at the stone. They heard him mutter, "No . . . no . . . it can't be . . ."

34

Brendan said, in a high, long–drawn–out moan, "Reveeeenge!"

Séamus stepped back further, and went very pale. He began to shake his head vigorously. "No . . . no . . . it wasn't me . . . I never touched you . . ." he babbled.

Then there was a high-pitched, sneering laugh that seemed to echo through the graveyard. Séamus screamed. There was a loud barking from up by the gate, then Lonnigan the Alsatian came bounding across the graveyard, trailing his lead which he'd snapped off.

Séamus had begun to stumble away from Sailor Jack's grave, but when Lonnigan reached him the dog stood on his hind legs and put his front paws on Séamus's shoulders and began licking his face.

Séamus lost his balance and fell backwards on to the ground. Lonnigan put his paws on his chest and continued licking his face.

"Lonnigan, get off, get off! Good boy!" wailed Séamus, trying to push the dog away. Finally Séamus sat up and, after a last lick, Lonnigan began to bark joyfully. Then he started to run around, sniffing. At Sailor Jack's grave, he burrowed into the hollow in the middle of the scattered stones, and came up with a bone in his jaws. He wagged his tail happily.

"No, Lonnigan, no!" cried Séamus. "Give it here! Drop it!"

"He thinks it's one of Sailor Jack's bones," whispered Brendan.

"And maybe it is," said Molly. They looked at each other in alarm. Séamus snatched the bone away from Lonnigan, and hastily crawled over to the grave and pushed it back into the hollow, covering it with earth.

Lonnigan began to bark, then he went sniffing around behind the tombstone. The snuffling Alsatian was only a foot or two from the wall and the bushes which hid Brendan and Molly. Now he was sniffing at the wall, and his head came over it. He seemed to be staring straight at the hidden pair. He began to bark loudly.

"Lonnigan, what is it? Come here, boy!" said Séamus, getting up and moving towards the dog. At any moment he would reach the wall and look into the bushes and see them. There was nothing they could do but stay still and hope.

Just then they heard a high, shrill whistle from up by the gate of the graveyard. The dog stopped barking and pricked up his ears, looking round. Séamus looked round too. There was no one to be seen at the gate, but they heard the whistle again.

Brendan realised it must be Dessy. He had seen that the dog had sniffed out their hiding-place, and was trying to distract his attention. A third whistle did the trick. Lonnigan gave a last bark, and then bounded across towards the gate, leaping over the graves as he went. Séamus stumbled after him.

When they reached the gate Lonnigan began sniffing around and jumping up and down. Séamus looked about, wondering where the whistle had come from. He obviously didn't see any sign of Dessy, and Molly and Brendan wondered where he had managed to hide. If he was nearby, Lonnigan would surely sniff him out.

Then they saw Séamus seize the snapped end of Lonnigan's lead, and pull him towards the Land-Rover. He bundled the dog into it and tied the lead to the door. With a last look back at the graveyard, he climbed into the driver's seat and started the engine. The Land-Rover moved away down the road.

Molly and Brendan looked at each other in relief. They had very nearly been discovered. Then they jumped as they heard a voice just beside them say, "Gotcha!"

It was Dessy. "Surprised you there, didn't I?" he smiled. "I'd be a great surprise attacker, so I would. I sneaked round through the woods behind the side wall of the graveyard to get out of the way of Séamus and that hideous hound. I realised where you must be hiding, and it looks like I whistled just in time."

"You sure did, thanks," said Brendan. They clambered out of the bushes and over the wall, and stood beside Sailor Jack's grave.

Molly told Dessy about Brendan's ghost-voice and how it frightened Séamus. "It was very risky," she said, "I thought Séamus might find us out, but Brendan fooled him. And the laugh he gave at the end was really spooky."

Brendan looked worried. "The laugh?" he said. "I didn't do that. I thought it was you."

"I never uttered a sound," said Molly.

"Well, don't look at me," said Dessy. "I gave the whistles, but spooky laughter's not my line."

"Then who was it?" asked Brendan.

They all turned and gazed at the grave of Sailor Jack.

Then they looked at one another grimly. *"Beware all who meddle with this noble grave . . ."* Brendan read from the inscription.

They stood silently for a few moments. The wind rustled in the trees, louder than before. But could they hear more than the wind?

A ghostly voice, laughing?

"It's time we got back," said Molly, "the Darlys are due to come for tea today."

"Yes, we'd better hurry," Brendan agreed, and with a last look back at Sailor Jack's grave, they went with grateful speed across to the gate, and took their bicycles out of the bushes.

When they got back to Ballygandon, they saw the Darlys' green car parked in the yard in front of the Donovans' shop. Beside it was Locky's old car.

As they got off their bikes, Locky himself came out of the house. "Good news, kids!" he called. "My horse did its stuff. A complete outsider, at a hundred to one. I can give you the money to get you to California!"

CHAPTER FIVE

Sky-high to America

"Dessy, they'll never let you into America if they see that photograph!" Brendan exclaimed, as they looked at their brand-new passports. Dessy's grinning face gazed at them from the page, his hair sticking up like a spiky crown.

"Yours is no better," said Dessy, "you're gawping like a half-witted clown."

"Well, I think I look quite good in mine," said Molly. "I wouldn't be surprised if a Hollywood talent scout spots me straight away."

Since Locky had given them the marvellous news about his win, they had been involved in hectic preparations for the trip. There were the passports and visas to be got, flight tickets arranged, money changed into dollars.

Their parents had had a meeting with Mrs Boyd, who said she would bring them to the airport and look after them all the way until Billy and his mother met them in Los Angeles. She would do the same on the way back.

They had said goodbye to the Darly family when they returned home, saying they would see them in California. They had spoken on the phone to Billy Bantam, who was very excited at the prospect of a reunion. He said he'd be there to meet them at the airport, and they could all stay in his mother's house in Beverly Hills, the place where so many of the big stars had homes. And they would be able to come to the studio and watch him filming his new movie.

The three of them were there when Locky rang Séamus Gallagher to tell him that Mrs Trout would not at present be continuing her search for her family's grave.

Locky held the receiver out and they could hear Séamus blustering angrily at the other end. "But I have already found the grave, and gone to great trouble and expense," he said. "Mrs Trout agreed to pay me, and I want my money."

"She agreed nothing," snapped Locky, "and you can go and whistle for your money."

"I'll have the law on you!" said Séamus, "Mister Fishface or whatever your name is."

"If it's law you want, you'd better watch out," said Locky. "If you're not careful the law may be doing some tracing on your Tree Tracing outfit."

"What?" cried Séamus, sounding alarmed. "What are you talking about?"

"I'll say no more," said Locky. "But just watch it. Or you may find some clever Private Eyes have got their eyes on you!" He put down the phone, and grinned at Molly, Brendan and Dessy. "That should have our friend Séamus sweating a bit."

"He'll sweat even more when we track down his partner in Los Angeles, and expose the whole business," said Brendan.

"According to the Tree Tracers brochure," said Molly, "this Doctor Galvin has an address in Santa Monica, and it looks from the map to be not far from Beverly Hills where Billy is."

"Just take a word of warning from your old grandfather, though," said Locky, "and promise you won't do anything rash. Séamus may be a bit of an eejit, but his mates at the American end could be a lot more ruthless if they see their business threatened."

"We'll be careful," said Molly.

Locky came to the airport with Brendan's parents to see them off. None of them had ever flown before. They were very excited, but a bit nervous too, though they didn't want to admit it. They looked at the red glowing lettering of the destinations board in the big hall with amazement. There were flights going to Paris, Moscow, Rome, Venice, Madrid . . . the names themselves were exciting.

Their own flight was to London where they would change to another plane for the long eleven-

41

hour flight to Los Angeles. Dublin airport was bustling with people, wheeling supermarket-style trolleys piled with cases and bags, and queueing at the check-in desks. The three of them joined the queue for the London plane with Mrs Boyd, clutching their tickets and passports.

When they reached the desk they were given their seat numbers and put their own luggage on a platform beside the desk. They each had a hold-all bag of a different colour. Dessy had put stick-on letters on his saying HOLLYWOOD, with little glittery stars stuck all around it.

"Everyone will know where *I'm* heading," he said, as he watched the bag go on to a moving belt with all the others, and disappear into the distance.

"How does the bag know to change planes in London on its own?" Molly wondered.

"It's all done with electronic tagging," said Brendan confidently, though he himself was amazed at the scale of the operation.

"Surely some bags must go to the wrong place?" Molly was worried that she would never see her new green hold-all again.

"It can happen," said Locky. "You know the old joke about modern travel: 'Breakfast in Dublin, lunch in New York, luggage in Hong Kong.'"

Molly looked worried. "I was only joking," said Locky, grinning.

At the entrance to the Departures area, Mrs Boyd

and the three travellers said goodbye to Brendan's parents and Locky. Brendan's mother hugged him tearfully, to Brendan's embarrassment, and said, "Look after yourself, won't you? And remember to wash your neck."

His father shook hands solemnly and said, "Good luck, son."

Locky gave them each a pat on the head, and said, "Say hello to California for me, and send us a postcard of the Empire State Building."

"That's in New York, Grandpa," Molly laughed.

"I was just testing you!" said Locky, as they went through the entrance, waving.

They had to put their hand luggage on a moving belt that went through a short tunnel to be X-rayed by a machine. Apart from Mrs Boyd, who had a handbag, Brendan was the only one with hand-luggage: a canvas bag with a football team logo on it, containing some comics and a plastic container with sandwiches for the journey. His mother insisted he should take them, though everyone said they were served great meals during the flight.

They had to take coins and keys and any other metal out of their pockets, then walk through an archway that had metal-detecting rays. As they went through they could see a TV screen which showed the X-ray of the bags going through the tunnel. The screen showed what was inside the bags, and the various objects glowed like pieces of a jumbled jigsaw.

Dessy was the last to go through the archway. As he went under it, there was a loud, electronic bleep.

"What have you got in your pockets, lad?" asked the uniformed man beside the archway.

"I guess it's just my trusty old forty-five-calibre pistol," said Dessy.

The man was not amused. "This is no joke," he said sternly. "We take security seriously here, young fella."

"Sorry," said Dessy sheepishly.

"So, what metal are you carrying?"

"Oh, I forgot," said Dessy, "it must be this." He produced a mobile phone from his pocket and gave it to the man. Then he was asked to go back through the archway, and walk through it again. This time, there was no electronic bleep.

"Right, off you go," said the uniformed man.

Dessy joined the others, who had collected their bags and were watching curiously.

"I didn't know you had one of those phones, Dessy," said Brendan with some envy.

"Oh, I like to keep in touch with headquarters," said Dessy, about to put the phone back in his pocket.

"Let's have a look," said Brendan. Dessy didn't want to hand it over, but Brendan was too quick for him, and grabbed the phone out of his hand.

"Don't mess it up," said Dessy. "Those yokes are very sensitive."

"Oh sure," said Brendan. He slid open the cover

44

of the instrument. There was nothing inside the casing. "It's just a toy," Brendan laughed.

"No, it's not, it's the real thing," said Dessy. "My brother gave it to me. It just hasn't got the inside wiring in yet."

Brendan decided not to inquire any further. Dessy's brother was a dodgy character whose activities often got him into trouble with the Guards. It would be better not to know just what lorry this particular bit of electronics had fallen from the back of.

Mrs Boyd said kindly, "Well, it looks like the real thing, anyway, Dessy. Now, let's make our way to the departure gate."

When their flight number was called, they filed through another archway and down a short tunnel which led to the door of the aircraft. Just beside the door on the side of the plane Brendan saw the name *Saint Jarlath* in green letters. "Who's Saint Jarlath?" he asked.

"I don't know," said Dessy, "but I'm with him all the way!"

The stewardess pointed them down the aisle to their seats. The three of them were in a row, with Molly in the window seat. Mrs Boyd was on the other side of the aisle.

They fastened their seat belts over their laps, and waited. Other passengers came in, peering around for their seat numbers and putting bags in the luggage compartments above the seats.

Finally the aircraft taxied slowly across to the runway, and they were ready for take-off. Molly peered out of the window as the engine roared and the tarmac runway started to move below, faster and faster, until suddenly it was getting further and further away as the plane rose into the air. Soon the cars and people and buildings below looked like little miniature toys, and the green fields spread out like a mosaic.

They crossed the coast and all three of them craned over to see what they could out of the window. It was like flying over a map.

"There's Ireland's Eye," said Molly.

"And that's Dún Laoghaire harbour over there," said Brendan.

"And there are the Pigeon House chimneys," said Dessy.

Soon they had left the coast behind and were flying over the sea, where tiny ships made their slow way through water that looked like a pond.

The cabin crew brought them biscuits and little sandwiches and soft drinks. Then they saw the coast of Wales, and it wasn't long before the captain was telling them they were about to land in Heathrow.

Here they had to change from one terminal building to another, to catch the plane for Los Angeles. There seemed to be endless walking down corridors and up and down stairs.

"We could have walked to America at this rate," said Dessy.

"Everyone says this is the worst part of air travel," said Mrs Boyd. "They have no problem whizzing us through the air, but no one has got the hang of moving people smoothly on the ground at airports."

Finally after a short bus journey they were in the right terminal, with a busy hallway like the one where they had started.

The plane was much bigger than the first one. It was a jumbo jet, and when they entered it they could see a spiral staircase leading up to the cabin on the upper deck.

"Who gets to go up there?" asked Brendan.

"The pilots, for a start," said Mrs Boyd, "and some passengers too. The rest of us are on the ground floor."

They settled into their seats, and this time Brendan was in the seat beside the window. He looked down as the runway seemed to begin to move beneath the giant aircraft. How could such a vast, heavy machine ever get off the ground, he wondered, as the plane lumbered along the tarmac, getting faster and faster. He had read about air speed and slipstreams and seen diagrams of how planes flew, but when you were sitting in this huge structure with hundreds of other people, it just didn't seem possible.

Yet here they were, airborne. He could see the ground once again getting further and further away, and the world below becoming tiny and distant. The great plane rose higher and higher and suddenly the view was blotted out by a white fog. Brendan realised they had flown into the clouds.

The whiteness continued to blot out the view for several minutes, then suddenly it disappeared and they were flying above the clouds, in bright sunlight. Brendan looked down.

It was an amazing sight: a landscape that looked like a vast carpet of cotton wool, or herds of white sheep crowded together. In the distance tall towers of cloud rose up into the air like soft skyscrapers. The sunlight glinted on the silver wing of the plane, whose engines had now settled to a steady, droning sound as they carried the machine through the sky towards America.

At one point, Brendan could see the shadow of the plane on the clouds below. It hardly seemed to be moving at all, and it was difficult to believe that they were actually travelling at a speed of hundreds of miles an hour.

A voice came through the plane's relay system. "Good afternoon, ladies and gentlemen, and welcome to our flight to Los Angeles. This is your captain, Jack Moran, speaking . . . "

As he went on to talk about their flight time and air speed and other details, Molly said, "Did you hear that? The pilot's called Jack Moran. The same name as Sailor Jack, back in Lisbeg graveyard."

"Bring back Saint Jarlath!" said Dessy.

CHAPTER SIX

Welcome to Hollywood

"Fasten your seat belts, please, we are preparing to land at Los Angeles airport . . ."

Dessy looked at his watch. "Hey, it's twelve o'clock at night back home," he said.

Brendan had adjusted his own watch to California time. "Here it's only four o'clock in the afternoon," he said. "We've stretched the day by eight hours."

"It's funny, but I don't feel tired," said Molly.

"Nor do I," said Dessy. "I can't wait to hit the bright lights of down-town LA!"

As the plane circled they looked down and saw the amazing city of Los Angeles spread out below. It seemed to stretch for ever, on all sides, only ending in the far misty distance where they could see the rolling breakers of the Pacific Ocean.

Everywhere there were roads, snaking and twisting and going over and under each other, with a continuous flow of cars on each one. Here and there amidst the road network were clusters of skyscrapers like people standing huddled together, rising up from the mass of smaller buildings. There was a scattering of bright blue circles and squares, the swimming pools in people's gardens.

Lower and lower they came until finally, with a slight bump and a roar of the engines, the huge plane was down on the runway and gradually slowing to a stop.

"Well, our pilot Sailor Jack got us safely into port," said Dessy.

They waited in the baggage hall where there were several carousels carrying a variety of luggage, from large metal boxes to golf clubs and strangely-shaped parcels, as well as suitcases and hold-alls.

A long-eared dog led by a man in uniform was sniffing at the bags as they went past. "Hello, boy!" said Molly, leaning forward to pat him.

"Don't distract him, young lady," said the uniformed man. "Robby here is a member of the Drug Squad. If there are any drugs hidden in those bags, he'll sniff them!"

Molly gazed at their flight's carousel anxiously. She wished Grandpa Locky hadn't made that joke about lunch in New York, luggage in Hong Kong. But suddenly she heard Dessy cry, "There it is!" as he pointed to his glittery bag with the stars stuck on to it. He leaned forward and grabbed it from the carousel. Soon Molly's hold-all and the rest of their bags appeared, and Mrs Boyd led the way with her trolley through the Customs area and out into the arrivals hall.

"Molly! Brendan! Dessy! Over here!" It was Billy Bantam's excited voice calling. They looked across at the crowd, and there at the front was Billy with his black wavy hair, wearing a smart green jacket. He was holding an Irish flag above his head. They rushed over to him eagerly and there were greetings and hugs and everyone was talking at once. Behind Billy stood a tall man in a black coat and a peaked cap, waiting patiently. They realised this must be Billy's chauffeur.

Mrs Boyd and a younger woman came over to them. Mrs Boyd introduced her daughter, and wished them a happy holiday. They thanked her for bringing them to California.

"It was a pleasure," said Mrs Boyd, "you were good company. And no trouble at all. I'll see you when we make the journey home."

The tall man in the cap said, "If you and your friends will wait outside there, I'll bring the car over."

He strode away and they pushed their trolley of bags across the hall. Several people recognised Billy and stopped him to ask for his autograph. He produced a batch of the sheets of paper with his picture on, like the one he'd sent with the letter to them all. He signed one for each of the autograph-hunters.

"You really are famous, Billy!" said Dessy.

"Well, when your joke routines make you a star, Dessy, you could be signing autographs yourself one day," said Billy, slapping Dessy on the back.

They went out of the door on to a footpath beside a road. It was lined with people getting into cars and coaches.

"Wow, it's hot," said Molly.

"It's like this all the time," said Billy. "I prefer Ireland where you get those 'soft days', as you call them."

"Which really means it's drizzling rain," said Brendan.

"It makes a nice change," said Billy. "Still, when you get home to our house you'll have the pool to cool off in."

"You've got your own pool?" asked Molly.

"Oh sure, most people do in Beverly Hills," said Billy. "We're having a pool party tomorrow. Here's the car."

The three of them stared in amazement as the longest car they had ever seen purred to a halt beside them. It was white and polished, and seemed to be as long as two ordinary cars stuck together.

The driver got out and started to pick up their bags. "I'll put these in the trunk," he said.

Brendan thought it was odd to put one lot of luggage into another piece of luggage, then he remembered that when Americans said *trunk* they meant *boot*. Which, when you came to think of it, was an even odder word, as if you put suitcases into your shoe.

"Aren't you going to come with us, Brendan?" Molly was leaning out of the window of the limousine. While Brendan had been daydreaming, they had all got into the car. He climbed in himself, and sat down on a soft leather seat beside Dessy. They had their backs to the driver, and Billy and Molly were on the back seat of the car, facing them. There was so much space between the seats that they could all stretch out their legs full-length, without touching the foot of the person opposite.

Along the side of the car beside the arm-rest Brendan saw a rack of glasses and a decanter. Billy pointed at them and said, "I wanted to greet you with champagne, but my mom said no. It's just lemonade, but let's drink a toast to your arrival anyway."

He poured out drinks and they raised their glasses. "California, here we come!" said Dessy.

"Happy days!" said Billy, and they clinked their glasses together.

It seemed odd at first that the traffic drove on the right. The long limo moved smoothly along the roads, joining and leaving freeways with five lanes of traffic on each side. Finally they were in a wide road with palm trees beside it, and big houses behind walls. "This is Sunset Boulevard," said Billy. "We'll soon be home."

They went up a hill into a leafy road and stopped outside a big security gate set into a high brick wall. Brendan saw a large metal shield stuck on to the wall, with brass lettering that said: ARMED RESPONSE. "What does that mean?" he asked.

"Everyone has it around here," said Billy. "You have to. It means we're automatically linked to a security firm's headquarters, so if there's a break-in and an alarm goes off, guys with guns are here in a minute to deal with it."

Brendan wasn't sure if knowing that made him feel safer or more nervous.

The driver pointed a gadget like a TV remote control at the side of the gate. There was a buzz, and the double gates opened automatically. The car moved through and the gates closed behind. They went up a winding driveway past neatly-cut lawns and palm trees and big bushes with red and white flowers on them.

The car drew up at the front entrance of a very big house. There were white pillars beside steps that led up to a verandah and polished wood double doors with brass knockers on them, shaped like dolphins. Billy's father, a rich film producer, had built this mansion. But he died when Billy was only six, and since then Billy and his mother had continued to live here in real Hollywood style.

The driver got the bags out, and they thanked him. A young man only a few years older than they were appeared. He too was in uniform, a dark blue outfit with a waistcoat, and trousers with a gold stripe down the side.

"Hi, Jim," said Billy, "could you take my friends' bags to their rooms?"

"Sure," said Jim, picking the bags up. As they went up the steps Billy's mother came out of the big doors to greet them.

"Well, hi there, welcome to California!" she cried, holding out her arms to embrace them all, the bracelets on her wrists jangling and clinking as she hugged them one by one. "My, I think you've grown since I last saw you in Ireland!"

Brendan always wondered why adults seemed surprised to see that people had got taller. It was almost as if they expected them to have got smaller, like the hero of a film Brendan had once seen, *The Incredible Shrinking Man*. When he was watching movies like that, he never imagined he would ever be here in Hollywood, where they were actually made.

Molly had a room of her own, and Brendan and Dessy were sharing a big, airy room with a tiled floor and its own bathroom, and windows that looked out on the swimming-pool. There were chairs and tables around the pool, and umbrellas against the sun, as well as palm trees. It looked exactly like the scenes you so often saw in the movies. But in those, there was frequently a bloodstained body floating in the pool.

Fortunately this pool didn't have a corpse in it, and it wasn't long before Brendan, Dessy and Molly were in it themselves, splashing around and swimming, and climbing out to sit in the poolside chairs sipping iced lemonade.

"It's just great to see the Ballygandon Gang here in Hollywood," said Billy. "I knew you'd get here some day, I just knew it."

"It's great to be here," said Molly.

"Now tell me what you've been up to since I was in Ireland," said Billy. "Have they made any more movies round Ballygandon?"

"No, our film career started and stopped at the same time, it seems," said Brendan.

"But now we're in Hollywood, who knows what could happen?" said Dessy.

"Anything can happen in the movie business," said Billy, "it's a crazy world. This one I'm in now is about the French Revolution, with lots of sword fights and fancy costumes. I play a boy aristocrat who is going to be beheaded by the guillotine, but a faithful servant rides in disguised as a soldier and saves me at the last minute. While you're here I'll arrange for you to come on the set and see it."

"I'd love to see a real film studio," said Molly.

"I've got an idea," said Billy. "Tomorrow I've got to work out of town on location, but you could see a studio yourselves. There's a tour of some studios you can go on. They show you all the tricks of the trade, monsters, floods, earthquakes and avalanches – all kinds of stunts. Mom will take you, won't you, Mom?"

He called over to his mother who was dozing in a long deck-chair. She was tall and blonde and was wearing a big red straw hat and an oriental silk dressing-gown over her swimsuit. She had sunglasses with glittery jewels on the rims.

"Of course, I'd be glad to take you," she said. "I love going to the studios. It reminds me of my actress days. Now don't you forget, Billy, you're to go to bed early. The studio car is calling for you at five."

"Five in the morning?" asked Brendan, startled.

"Sure, I often start that early," said Billy.

"I didn't know filming was such hard work in Hollywood," said Brendan. He began to wonder if a career in the movies would be such a doddle, after all.

They asked Billy about Santa Monica, where the Tree Tracers partner Doctor Galvin was based. He told them it was a city not far away, on the coast. It was a posh area to live.

"It's a city, is it?" asked Molly. "I thought it was part of Los Angeles."

"The whole place is really lots of cities joined together," said Billy. "Tell me about this Tree Tracer person, is she a friend of yours?"

They explained about the arrival of the Darlys to look for their family grave, and how Séamus Gallagher was involved in faking names for people sent over by his partner here in California.

"That's a dirty trick," said Billy. "We'll have to check out this partner. Maybe I can pretend to be looking for *my* roots, and sign up as a client."

They discussed this plan excitedly. Doctor

Galvin would not be suspicious of a real American making inquiries. Molly wondered what Séamus could do about the name *Bantam*. Would he find a *Banham*, perhaps, or a *Banahan*, or even a *Barnum*, like the circus. What was it called? *Barnum and Bailey* . . . ?

"Molly, wake up!" she heard Brendan's voice say sharply. Only then did she realise she had closed her eyes and dozed off while she was thinking of the list of names. Her head had slumped forward on her shoulders and she had been really sleeping.

"I suppose it's not surprising," said Dessy, looking at his watch. "After all, it *is* three o'clock in the morning."

"You'll have to change that watch to California time," said Brendan, "otherwise we'll all be totally confused."

He found himself yawning. When Dessy told him what time it really was, he realised how long they had been awake. It seemed days since they had left Dublin.

Now Dessy was yawning too.

"Jet-lag, that's what it is," said Billy's mother. "Just time for a quick snack, and then it's into bed for all of you."

CHAPTER SEVEN

Cowboy Dessy

On the way to the studio tour in the giant limo, Mrs Bantam pointed out the hill with the famous sign in huge letters that said HOLLYWOOD, and they saw over a large arched gateway the carved face of the MGM Lion which they had watched roaring at the beginning of so many films.

"That lion came from Dublin Zoo," said Brendan.

"You're joking me," said Dessy.

"It's a known fact," Brendan declared. "Grandpa Locky told me. They were looking all over the world for just the right lion to do the roaring, and they found him at Dublin Zoo. He was called Stephen."

"Yes, Grandpa told *us* that too," said Molly. "I'm sure you've heard it, Mrs Bantam?"

Billy's mother looked uncertain. "Well," she said, "I was never sure exactly where they got the lion, but it could well be Stephen, I suppose. Perhaps he roars with a Dublin accent."

"Like me!" said Dessy, giving out a loud howling roar that startled everyone including the driver, who glanced round in alarm.

As they waited at the entrance to the studio for the tour to begin, Dessy was startled when he was given a friendly handshake by a towering figure that looked like one of the creatures created by Doctor Frankenstein.

They travelled in a special tram that took them through a fantasy world of film sets. At each stop they were shown spectacular special effects. Once, with a crash and a thunderous roar, a whole mountain seemed to crumble and fall down on top of them, with rocks and stones hurtling all around.

In another place, a flash flood seemed to engulf them, as tons of water washed away buildings and it looked as if the tram would be drowned by the tumbling waves. But suddenly the taps behind the scenes were turned off, the water drained away, the buildings righted themselves and the whole set looked just as it had before.

Then the guide pointed out another tram which was just crossing a river. Before their eyes, the bridge seemed to collapse and the tram sank into the water.

"That could have been us!" said Dessy, alarmed.

"It will be," said the guide. They looked at the tram which had somehow appeared dry and intact on the far side of the river. Their own tram moved on to the restored bridge, and when the guide gave the signal, the bridge tilted forward and the tram rolled down the rails. They entered a cutting and then a special tunnel which went underneath the river and came out at the other side. To the onlookers in the following tram, it looked as if they had disappeared into the water.

They watched a house engulfed by a raging fire, which stood unharmed when the flame jets were turned off. They trundled past a lake and gasped when a huge shark suddenly leaped out of it like a rocket.

Then they were shown into rows of seats beside a dusty arena. On the far side were wooden buildings that looked like the street scene in so many Western movies. There were the saloon and the general store and the bank and the sheriff's office and the jail.

They expected to see cowboys ride in on horses at any moment. And that was exactly what happened. The horses pulled up in the square, and four of the cowboys hitched them to the rail outside the saloon bar and went inside. Soon there was the sound of gunfire, and two of the cowboys came staggering out through the swing-doors and fell dead on the square. A sleek cigar-smoking man in a black suit and wearing a black stetson hat came out of the saloon, a gun in his hand.

He looked around. Two cowboys ran out of the saloon and tried to reach their horses, but the man in black fired at them, and they ducked into the general store. The man in black followed them, and soon the cowboys appeared on the roof of the building. A shot rang out, and one of the cowboys cried out, raised his arms, and fell forward off the roof, plunging to the street below.

The audience gasped. Brendan said, "Look, there's a mattress in the street." Indeed, they could see that the cowboy had fallen on to a giant version of the kind of cushioned mattress they had seen pole-vaulters and high-jumpers land on in the Olympic Games.

The chase continued, as more cowboys arrived on the scene, and stunt-men tumbled from the roof down on to the mattress below. Suddenly Brendan said, "Where's Dessy?"

"I don't know," said Molly, "maybe he went for a pee. I mean," she added, glancing at Mrs Bantam, "perhaps he went to the toilet."

"Look up there!" cried Brendan, pointing at the roof of the film set. Beside the two cowboys who were now having a wrestling match on the roof, a small figure with spiky hair had appeared.

It was Dessy. The wrestling actors were too busy to see him, but the man in black who was in the arena and about to shoot at the cowboys up on the roof, shouted, "Hey, what's that kid doing up there?"

There was a murmur of surprise from the audience, and a man with a megaphone and a peaked cap called, "Keep calm, boy. Just stay exactly where you are."

"How did he get up there?" asked Mrs Bantam.

"He must have sneaked round the back of the scenery, and just climbed up," said Molly.

The two wrestling cowboys on the roof heard the megaphone and realised something odd was happening. They stopped fighting and turned and saw Dessy. One of them moved across towards him. Dessy peered over the edge of the roof uncertainly. Then he hurled himself off.

He seemed to do a somersault in the air, curled up in a crouching position. Then he landed on his back on the big mattress. He lay there for a moment, while Brendan and Molly stood up to look over the heads of the audience. They were just about to run forward into the arena when Dessy stood up, swaying a bit on the spongy mattress, and held his arms up in the air.

There was a cheer from the crowd, and Dessy stepped off the mattress into the arena. The megaphone man and other official-looking people gathered round him. One of them called over a nurse who was standing by. Mrs Bantam and Molly and Brendan got up from their seats and pushed through the crowd into the arena.

They found Dessy in the centre of a hubbub of noise and shouting, with people asking if he was all right and others haranguing him for being reckless and foolish.

"Pardon me!" Mrs Bantam's sharp voice cut through the racket like a knife. There was a silence while everyone looked her way. "This young man is with me," Mrs Bantam went on. "He is a visitor from Ireland, and I guess he didn't quite understand that this was not an interactive programme in which he could participate."

The officials looked baffled by this elaborate description of Dessy's little escapade. If they planned any further action against him, they didn't have time to pursue it. Mrs Bantam reached forward, took Dessy's hand, and led him firmly away from the throng. "Which way is the exit, please?" she demanded.

They settled down to drink milk-shakes in a café near the exit, while Mrs Bantam contacted the driver on her mobile phone and said they were ready to be collected. Then she turned to Dessy and told him off sharply for being so rash.

"If you take any more risks like that, I'll have to send you home at once," she said. But nevertheless she smiled and nodded graciously as people from the audience came up and congratulated Dessy on his performance. A few of them even asked for his autograph, and Dessy signed his name with a flourish.

"I could get used to this," he said.

"We might as well do some writing too," said Brendan, producing a postcard. "I'm going to write to Locky and thank him for getting us here."

"Tell him our friend's ham-acting nearly got us sent straight back," said Molly.

"No, don't do that," said Dessy.

"OK," said Brendan, "I'll just write: *Dessy has landed . . . on his feet.*"

That afternoon at the pool party, they had the strange sense of having met a lot of the people before. But in fact the people who looked so familiar were faces they had seen on the cinema screen. All of them greeted Billy warmly, as an equal star, and were very welcoming when he introduced his three friends.

"They were in a movie with me in Ireland," he said casually, and the three of them felt almost as if they were stars themselves.

Brad and Grace Darly arrived and showed them an elaborate scroll on parchment-like paper, with the Darly family tree with lots of names on it in old-fashioned lettering.

"Tree Tracers sent us this," said Grace. "Mom and Dad asked us to show it to you."

"It looks to me just like some kind of fancy telephone directory," said Brad. "I'm more interested in the future than all this historical stuff."

"It's important to Mom and Dad," said Grace.

Brendan wondered whether they should warn the Darlys about Tree Tracers, but they had spent the money now and it seemed a pity to disappoint them. He didn't think Brad and Grace would mind very much, but it would be a shock to their parents. They would have to know one day, when the

Ballygandon Gang exposed Séamus Gallagher and his activities, but there was a fair bit of investigating to do before that revelation was made.

The investigation began the next day. Billy had a day off from filming, and at lunch-time they headed towards Santa Monica in the white limousine. Brendan was getting quite used to this form of transport. He wondered what they would say at home if he arrived in the limo. It would practically take up the whole street, and in the city you would probably need two or three parking-meter spaces to park it.

At Santa Monica they had a picnic on the huge sandy beach fringed by palm-trees. At the back of the beach there was a path crowded with joggers, roller-bladers, skateboarders and bike riders. They walked down towards the pier that jutted out into the ocean, and saw a group of people who made their eyes widen in astonishment.

They were energetically heaving weights and bars up and down, doing push-ups on mats, and swinging on high rails. Their arms and chests and legs were bulging with huge muscles and glistening with oil or maybe sweat.

"They call this Muscle Beach," said Billy.

"I can see why," said Brendan.

Billy had made an appointment to see Doctor Galvin in her office on Santa Monica Boulevard.

Her secretary had been impressed when he gave her his name.

"Are you *the* Billy Bantam, the film star?" she asked.

"That's me," said Billy.

"Well, I'll be *so* charmed to meet you, and so will Doctor Galvin," the secretary said.

The secretary did indeed seem charmed. When they entered the elegant office on the eighteenth floor, she came forward to greet them, her long eyelashes fluttering.

"And your friends are from *Ireland*!" she exclaimed when Billy introduced them. She sounded as amazed as if he had said they had just arrived from Mars.

They waited for a few minutes in the outer office, looking at the glossy photographs on the walls showing Irish beauty-spots, and imposing family trees. There were shields too, with the names of Irish families. The window looked out on the rolling breakers of the Pacific Ocean.

Molly gazed out, thinking that for thousands of miles there was nothing but sea and a few islands, till eventually you reached Australia.

There was a buzz from the secretary's desk, and she picked up the phone. Then she said, "Doctor Galvin will see you now."

She opened a door that led into another large and elegant office. There were armchairs and couches and a glass coffee-table with magazines on it. At the far end from the door was a big polished wood desk with a green leather top. A red and a white telephone stood on it, as well as neat filing trays. Beside it on a separate table stood a computer. There were framed certificates on the walls, saying that Doctor Galvin had received various degrees and awards.

Doctor Galvin got up and came round the desk to greet them. She was a woman of about thirty-five, wearing a well-cut expensive-looking emerald green suit, with a Celtic brooch on the lapel. Her hair was a glossy bronze colour, beautifully styled. This was definitely the more stylish branch of the firm of Tree Tracers, thought Molly.

"Dervla Galvin," the woman said, holding out her hand towards Billy. "You are very welcome to Tree Tracers. We have a number of stars whose ancestry we have been able to trace. We shall be happy to be of service to you."

Molly was startled. She had expected Doctor Galvin to be an American, but she spoke with an accent that would not have sounded out of place in Ballygandon itself.

Then she remembered. A couple of years ago there had been a local scandal in the village of Killbreen, near Ballygandon. A number of thefts had taken place in the area, mostly of jewellery and antiques. Some of them had then turned up for sale at a shop in the big town.

One of the people who ran the shop was none other than Séamus Gallagher's daughter, Dervla.

CHAPTER EIGHT

Discoveries

Molly remembered her parents talking about it all. Dervla Gallagher had claimed that she had been sold the jewellery and antiques by someone called Harry Galvin, but no such person could be traced. Nothing was ever proved, but soon afterwards Dervla had disappeared from the area.

No one knew what had happened to her, and Séamus used to tell people she had got an important job abroad, though he never said where. Now it looked as if they had found out.

Billy was introducing his three friends. "And what part of Ireland are you from?" Dervla asked.

"We're all from Dublin," said Molly hastily. She didn't want Dervla to connect her with Ballygandon. The other three looked at Molly curiously.

Brendan realised she must have a good reason for the deception. "Yes, from Dublin," he said.

Dervla began to tell Billy about Tree Tracers and their great success in tracking down people's Irish roots and family trees. She showed him a glossy book with pictures of shields and family crests.

"There's *your* name, Molly," said Billy suddenly. "Look – Donovan. It says the Donovans were chieftains in Munster, a thousand years ago."

"It's a well-known name in the part of Ireland where my partner, Mr Gallagher, is based," said Dervla. She looked at Molly with a puzzled expression, and said, "But you say your family is from Dublin?"

"That's right," said Molly. She saw that Dervla was still eyeing her with interest. Molly was afraid that before long Dervla might realise that she was indeed one of the local Donovans from Ballygandon, and become suspicious.

"Excuse me, Doctor Galvin," Molly said, "may I go to the Rest Room?" Though it seemed an odd thing to call it, Molly had learned that this was a word the Americans used for lavatory. She was anxious to get out of Dervla's way.

"Of course," Dervla said. "My secretary Janice will show you where it is."

Molly went back into the outer office, and Janice showed her the door that led from there into a small bathroom.

"I have to go down to the mail room," said Janice, "I guess you can find your way back?"

She smiled, and Molly smiled back and said, "Sure."

Janice went out. Molly wondered what to do. She didn't want to go back into the main office and risk Dervla realising who she was. Yet she couldn't stay away too long. She listened at the door of Dervla's office and heard her say, "I'll just ring my partner in Ireland and see what he feels the chances are of tracing the name Bantam there. I'm sure he'll be hopeful."

Molly was sure he would be, too. She doubted if there were any names Séamus wouldn't pretend to trace, if there was money to be had for doing it.

"Hello, Mr Gallagher," Molly heard Dervla say. "I'm here with a young client who is anxious to trace his family . . ."

Molly looked at the secretary's desk, which had a red and a white telephone on it, like those in Dervla's office. She realised that she would be able to listen in and hear the whole conversation. Carefully she picked up the white phone. She could hear Séamus Gallagher's voice as well as Dervla's.

"Well done, Dervla," he said. "Who have you got this time? I did a great job with those Darlys. I had them totally fooled."

"Yes, you did, thank you," said Dervla. "The young man I have here just now is a film star."

"Nice work, girl," said Séamus. "We should be able to milk him for a few bob."

Dervla kept up her formal tone so that the trio sitting opposite her wouldn't realise the kind of remarks Séamus was making.

"That's right," she said. "His name is Bantam. Billy Bantam." There was a long silence. "Hello, Mr Gallagher, are you still there?" said Dervla.

"I'm here all right," said Séamus, but now he sounded far less cheerful.

"Well, what do you think?" asked Dervla.

"He can't hear me, can he?" said Séamus.

"No, that's all right."

"Well, listen to me carefully. That boy could be trouble. Tell him you can't help him."

"I don't quite understand," said Dervla.

"Don't send him to me, whatever you do," said Séamus. "He'll recognise me. He was here making that werewolf film, the time I nearly got caught setting fire to the scenery. That Donovan girl and her friends were great mates of his, and they very nearly got me jailed. Luckily they couldn't prove it for certain."

Molly heard a note of alarm come into Dervla's voice, as she said, "What name did you say?"

"Donovan," said Séamus. "You know, the people who run that shop over in Ballygandon."

Now there was a silence at Dervla's end. Molly wondered what Dervla would do. Finally she said abruptly, "Thank you very much, I shall tell them." She put down the phone, and Molly carefully replaced the secretary's telephone too. She listened at the door of the main office.

"I am sorry, Mr Bantam," said Dervla coolly. "My partner says that unfortunately he can't help you. He has checked his computer listings, and finds that there is no record of your name anywhere in Ireland."

"But you just said you were sure . . ." said Billy.

"I know, but I was wrong, I'm afraid. There's nothing we can do to help you. Your name must have some other European origin. Now, if you'll excuse me, I have to make some further phone calls. Perhaps you will collect your friend Miss Donovan on the way out." Molly felt there was a particular coldness about the way Dervla said the name "Donovan".

Molly stepped away from the door. It opened and Dervla said, "Goodbye to you," as Billy, Brendan and Dessy came through into the outer office. The door closed.

"Say, that was a sudden turn-around," said Billy.

Molly lowered her voice and said, "Séamus has found us out. I listened in on the phone out here. Janice went out of the office for a while."

The telephone rang, and they heard Dervla in the other office say, "Yes? Oh, hello, it's you."

Molly put her finger to her lips, and went across to the secretary's desk. Once again she carefully picked up the white telephone and put it to her ear.

She heard Séamus say, "Have you got rid of them?"

"Yes, Dad, they've gone," said Dervla. Brendan, Dessy and Billy heard her say the word *Dad* and looked very startled. They glanced across at Molly, and she nodded.

Then she heard Séamus say, "That lot are real trouble, believe me. If he comes over here he's bound to link up with them, and they'll start meddling in our business."

"The Donovan girl was here with Billy Bantam. So were her two friends," said Dervla.

"WHAT?" Molly thought Séamus was going to explode. "What are those kids doing over there in Hollywood?"

"Visiting Billy Bantam, I guess."

"Well, steer clear of them. For all I know they may suspect something already. You didn't give anything away?"

"No, I just choked them off. I didn't tell them you were my father. Just called you my partner, like we agreed. I don't think they suspected anything."

"Well, make sure you have nothing more to do with them," said Séamus. "They're bad news."

Just then they heard the handle turn on the main door. Molly quickly put the phone down and came away from the desk. Janice came in.

"We're just leaving," said Billy Bantam.

"Well, it's been good to meet you," said Janice, simpering. "I am truly a great admirer of yours. I hope we may see you again when Doctor Galvin starts tracing your family."

"You never know," said Billy, as they went out into the corridor.

On the way back in the limousine, Molly told them what she had heard on the phone.

"Well, so much for my Irish roots!" said Billy. "I was rather hoping I might turn out to have some real Irish ancestors. The O'Bantams, perhaps."

"You certainly wouldn't find any real ones through Séamus or his daughter," said Molly. She told the others about the thefts and the scandal that had happened a couple of years before.

"She certainly seems to have taken after her father," said Brendan.

"And that's where she got the name Galvin, from that Harry Galvin she said she got the stuff from," said Dessy.

"I don't think there ever was a Harry Galvin," said Molly, "any more than there is a real *Doctor* Galvin. I'm sure the Doctor part of it is as fake as the surname."

"I suppose it impresses the punters," said Brendan.

"It certainly seems to pay dividends," said Billy, "judging by her plush office and all the trimmings there."

"She doesn't deserve to get away with it," said Molly. "There must be lots and lots of people who've parted with their money for a fake family tree."

"Not to mention a fake grave," said Dessy.

"Why don't we try scaring her?" asked Brendan. "We could ring up and tell her the FBI are investigating her."

The next day they got up really early and went to the studio to watch Billy filming. They saw him dressed up in his aristocrat's costume, with a beautiful patterned silk coat and knee-breeches and shoes with silver buckles. He had to run down a corridor while his pursuers were pounding at the door.

As usual, the scene had to be repeated several times until the director was satisfied with it. Between each take the make-up artist and the wardrobe mistress rushed up to Billy and made sure that he was tidied up properly.

Finally the director said, "OK, that's fine. We'll print it."

His assistant called, "Set up for Scene 45." People began to move scenery and cameras and lights. Billy came across to where his friends were standing, behind the camera. They congratulated him.

"You looked really scared," said Brendan.

"I imagined I was running away from Doctor Galvin," Billy laughed. Since he was not in the next scene, they went to his dressing-room. It had his name in silver letters on the door, and inside it was almost like a small flat, with a dressing-table with bright lights on it, a couch and armchairs, a cupboard full of costumes, and a shower.

They sipped cans of Coke while Billy started to look at the script for his next scene. Then he said, "Talking of Doctor Galvin, why don't we make that phone call now?" He produced his mobile phone.

"Shall I pretend to be the FBI?" asked Dessy.

"Your American accent is as phoney as her family trees," said Brendan.

"I guess I'd better do it," said Billy. Molly got out a copy of the Tree Tracers brochure and looked up the number. Billy dialled. Then, making his voice as deep as he could, he said, "Good afternoon, could I speak to Doctor Galvin, please?"

He listened for a short time, then said, "I see." He looked puzzled and frowned. Then he said, "I'll get back to you." He clicked the phone off and said, "Maybe we've scared her off already. Her secretary said she is away from the office for a while. She's going to Ireland on business."

They realised their investigations would have to wait until they got home. Back at Billy's house they told Mrs Bantam what they had been doing, and she wondered if they could set some real detectives on to the case.

"*We're* real detectives, or as good as," said Dessy. "We're the Ballygandon Private Eyes."

"The problem is," said Molly, "our cover is blown. Séamus and Dervla know we are on to them.

The chances are they will try to cover their tracks. We really need to have another go at luring them into some ancestor-tracing which we can expose, so we can catch them red-handed."

"But who can we get to pretend to be looking for their ancestors?"

"Will *I* do?" asked Mrs Bantam.

CHAPTER NINE

Computer Clues

Molly said, "That's wonderful, Mrs Bantam. Would you really come to Ireland and pretend to be looking for your ancestors?"

"Of course I will," said Billy's mother, "I just loved your beautiful country on my last visit, and this time I'll have a chance to perform, as well."

"That's great, Mom," said Billy, "but we'll have to think of a different name. Dervla knows ours already."

"Let me think," said Billy's mother. "My mother's name was Morgan. What about that?"

"It sounds OK to me," said Brendan.

"It's a Welsh name, you know," said Mrs Bantam. "My mother even taught me some Welsh. Songs, mainly." She began to sing vigorously in Welsh, in a high soprano voice.

"Thanks, Mom," Billy interrupted. "Don't get carried away."

"I'll be so glad to help," said Mrs Bantam, "and

the sooner the better, don't you think? Let me see, when are you going back to Ireland?"

"In a week's time," said Molly.

"Then why don't I come with you?"

The week was a hectic one. They spent two more days at the studio watching Billy. In one scene he was dressed in the ragged remnants of his fancy costume, having been kept in prison awaiting the guillotine. A number of extras hadn't turned up so, at Billy's suggestion, the director told Brendan, Dessy and Molly to go to Wardrobe and be fitted out with costumes. Now they were part of the crowd watching the executions.

They saw the guillotine being tried out with a false body. The blade crashed down with a whistling metallic sound, and sliced right through the neck. Fake blood spurted, and the head fell into a basket.

"Yuk!" said Molly.

"Hey," said Dessy, "do you know what the executioner said to the aristocrat?"

"What?" asked Brendan.

"Keep calm, and don't lose your head."

"That's grisly," said Molly.

"As the man said when he met a bear in the forest," Dessy laughed.

"What are those old women doing, sitting near the guillotine and knitting?" asked Brendan.

"That's what people used to do, apparently,"

said Billy. "They thought the guillotine was great entertainment."

"My mother knits when she's watching the telly," said Molly.

"It's sometimes just as violent," Dessy said.

"Places, please, for Scene 96," called the director's assistant.

Billy stood in line for the guillotine. Just as he was about to be led forward, a horseman rode in and swooped him up into the saddle.

"Cut!" the director cried. There was something he wasn't happy about, so they did the scene again – and then again. Once more, Brendan thought how strange the movie industry was. It was so odd to find an activity which was both very glamorous and very boring at the same time.

When the scene was finally finished, Billy came across to them. "Phew! That was exhausting," he said. "But you three certainly looked the part. A real bloodthirsty bunch of kids!"

"I hope your mother will enjoy acting the part of Mrs Morgan as much when we get back to Ireland, Billy," said Molly.

"Oh, she will," said Billy, "and she's really very good at it. It will be like the old days for her."

"I've been thinking," said Brendan. "Before we go back, do you think we should pay Doctor Galvin another visit and see what we can find out?"

"But she isn't there," said Dessy.

"Exactly!" said Brendan.

They called unannounced at the Tree Tracers office in Santa Monica.

"Oh, hello again!" said Janice the secretary, delighted to see one of her favourite stars once more. "I'm afraid Doctor Galvin isn't here. She had to go to Ireland rather suddenly on business."

"There's no rush," said Billy, "I'll contact her some other time. But meanwhile, I think I may have left a notebook in her office. I wonder if I could have a look?"

"Of course, come through," said Janice, opening the door to the inner office. They all went in. They had wondered if they would find the office cleared out, with "Doctor Galvin" having de-camped, afraid her frauds had been found out. But everything looked the same. She must be planning to return and carry on as before. That woman has quite a nerve, thought Molly.

They hoped Janice might leave them there or be called away, so they could have a quick look at the files for evidence. But she just stood there beaming, as Billy pretended to look for his notebook on the desk and the floor.

"I'm sure I had it here, but I can't see it," he said.

Then Brendan had an idea. He pointed at the computer beside the desk and said, "That looks a marvellous machine, much more advanced than we have at home, I'm sure."

"Oh, they're wonderful gadgets, aren't they?"

said Janice proudly. "I just don't know what we'd do without them. Do you know, we have thousands of names stored in there, all filed and cross-referenced. Doctor Galvin can track down any name you care to mention. It's just amazing how many people's names turn out to have an Irish background."

"Amazing!" said Molly.

"Can we see it working?" said Brendan eagerly.

"Why not? I'm sure Doctor Galvin wouldn't mind," said Janice.

Brendan wasn't sure at all, but he didn't say so. Instead he gathered round with the others while Janice sat at the computer and tapped the keys. A list came up on the screen:

Abbot

Acton

Adams

Adamson

"That's the basic list of common Irish names," said Janice, "there are thousands and thousands of them in there."

"Megabytes," said Dessy, "as the computer said when it sat down to a ten-course dinner."

Janice tapped the keys again, and said, "Now, let me see. This is a catalogue of graveyards, with all the names on the tombstones." She began to scroll through the lists. Molly saw that most of the graveyards were in the same county as Ballygandon

83

and Killbreen. It was obviously easier for Séamus to operate near home.

When the name *LISBEG* came on to the screen, Molly said, "I know someone in my mother's family is buried there, but I can't remember the name. Do you think I could have the list to show to her?"

"Sure, no problem," said Janice, and pressed a series of keys. A printer beside the computer began to whirr and stutter. Then it began to feed out pages. There were five altogether. Janice clipped them together and handed them to Molly.

Molly thanked her, and Janice said, "You're welcome. Now let's see if we can find that notebook." She switched off the computer and began shifting papers and searching.

"I guess I must have left it somewhere else," said Billy. "Thank you for your trouble."

"You're welcome," said Janice again, "and before you go, could I ask you a special favour?"

"Sure," said Billy.

"Could I have your autograph?"

"I wonder why she didn't ask for mine," said Dessy as they travelled back in the limo.

"I can't think," said Brendan. "Maybe she thought you didn't look as if you could write your name."

"Look at all *these* names," said Molly, scanning the print-out list. "Everyone in Lisbeg graveyard must be here."

"Including Sailor Jack?" asked Brendan.

"Yes, he's here," said Molly, "and look, here's the name *Daly*. It's got a little star against it."

"That's the one Séamus changed for the Darlys," said Brendan. "Perhaps the little star means he's used that one up."

"There are quite a few little stars," said Molly. "Séamus has been busy."

"When we get back," said Brendan, we can check all the starred names and see how Séamus has altered them. Then I can photograph them as evidence."

Billy had to stay at home for the filming, but Mrs Bantam arranged for a friend to stay and look after him. She booked a ticket to Ireland on the same flight as the others were travelling on. She was constantly going through her vast wardrobe of clothes and asking them about what to pack.

"Do you think this is too showy?" she said, waving a red dress with an ostrich-feather collar.

"Much too showy," said Billy. "You're not expecting to find a stately home, Mom."

"Besides, you've got one of those already," said Molly. "This mansion is as grand as anything you'd find in Ireland."

"Well, thank you," said Mrs Bantam, and went on examining dresses. "How about this?" she said, waving a jewelled evening dress in bright yellow. "It would go well with this diamond tiara."

Molly thought she would be suggesting a Groucho Marx moustache next. They finally persuaded her that something a bit less extravagant would be more suitable.

The few days before they left were full of activity. They made a visit to Disneyland and tried out as much as they could pack in, from a trip up the Amazon with crocodiles and hippos to a ride on Space Mountain, a hectic roller-coaster ride mostly in the dark, which left them dizzy and delighted.

They went to an American football match and marvelled at the players dressed up like huge barging gladiators, the drum majorettes with their high kicks, as well as the marching bands and the general razzamatazz. Afterwards they bought souvenir footballers' helmets and shirts, and a football.

The journey back was stranger than the one coming out. They set off in the afternoon and flew east over the rocky deserts and on across the USA and north over the freezing Arctic lands of Canada. It got dark, but the night only lasted a few hours and they were able to watch the sun rise over the horizon and touch the clouds with pink and gold.

When they arrived in London, Dessy insisted on looking at his watch and telling them that it was still only two o'clock in the morning back in Los Angeles. It made them all feel tired. Then there was the last lap to Dublin, where Brendan's father met them. He was going to take Brendan and Dessy home, while Mrs Bantam had hired a limousine to give Molly a lift and to take her to the hotel in the town near Ballygandon where her parents would collect her.

"We'll see you in a couple of days," Brendan told Molly.

"You've only just touched down in Dublin, and you're off to the country before you've had time to draw breath," joked Brendan's father.

"We've got things to do," said Brendan.

"Urgent investigations," said Mrs Bantam, mysteriously.

"Of a very *grave* nature," said Dessy, with what he thought was a sinister smile.

Brendan's father looked perplexed. "Well, I hope you'll have time to tell us what you've been doing in California before you set off again," he said.

"Better than that," said Brendan, flourishing his camera. "I'll soon have an album of photographs of it all."

"Don't forget to bring your camera to Ballygandon," said Molly. "We've got a lot of pictures to take, remember."

Brendan's family were delighted with the presents he'd brought home: a cowboy hat, a necklace of gold stars, a bottle of bourbon whiskey, and a box of fortune cookies which had little messages about your future hidden inside them.

When Molly got home, her mother told her

there had been a telephone call for her from Grace Darly in California. They had just learned that their parents planned to buy an old ruined house in Ireland, and were thinking of doing it up as a heritage centre.

"I thought they said they were planning to ask Séamus Gallagher to run it for them," Molly's mother said. "Surely they don't mean that desperate Séamus Gallagher who runs the pub in Killbreen?"

Molly was very much afraid that was who they did mean.

CHAPTER TEN

Crooked Plans

"It can't be that Séamus Gallagher," said Molly's father, "he's hardly able to run a pub, let alone a heritage centre."

Molly said nothing. She knew that Séamus Gallagher was a lot more wily and cunning than her parents thought. She asked if she could ring the Darlys and find out more. When she got through, Grace told her that they were all coming to Ireland in two weeks' time, and nothing definite would be settled before then. But their choice to run the heritage centre was as Molly feared: the same Séamus Gallagher as had found the family grave for them.

When Brendan and Dessy arrived in Ballygandon, Molly told them the news.

"Time's running out," said Brendan. "We've got to expose Séamus before the Darlys do any deals with him."

They went to see Mrs Bantam who had registered

as "Mrs Morgan" in the Grand Hotel in town. She had a suite with a sitting-room as well as a bedroom, and from her windows they could see the nearby woods, and the river that ran on through the countryside to Ballygandon in the distance.

"Such beautiful scenery," said Mrs Bantam, "I don't wonder everyone wants to find roots in your marvellous country. Maybe we'll even track down some real Morgans."

They explained that they had to get things moving, and Mrs Bantam said, "Well, I'm raring to go. Why don't I call up Mr Gallagher right now?"

Before she dialled, they watched in amazement as Mrs Bantam first closed her eyes in deep concentration, rubbing her hands together. Then she got up and paced up and down the room, making some fluttery gestures with her hands.

"Just getting into the mood for the part," she said, as she saw them gazing at her in astonishment. "Now, here we go!"

When she got through, she spoke in a grand voice as if she was some visiting duchess or royal person, being gracious to the peasants. Molly realised the sense of Billy's warning to his mother not to overdo the acting. But it seemed that Séamus was totally convinced.

"He was charmed, utterly charmed," said Mrs Bantam. "He will come here tomorrow afternoon to take tea with me. He says he feels sure that he will be able to trace the Morgan family for me."

"Did he say anything about 'Doctor Galvin'?" asked Molly.

"No, he didn't mention her. As far as I could gather, he's coming on his own."

"I'm sure she's around somewhere," said Dessy.

"She's probably lying low," said Molly. "She knows that if she shows her face around here, there'll be people asking awkward questions, including the Guards. Remember all those thefts she was suspected of."

"I wish we could think of a way of being there to hear what he says to you, Mrs Bantam," said Brendan.

"Maybe there *is* a way," said Molly. "Couldn't we pretend to be your children?"

"That would really blow our cover," said Brendan. "He knows exactly who we are."

"Not if we wear those football helmets we got in California," said Molly. "He'd think we were all-American kids."

"Just watch me be the linebacker making a twenty-yard dash," said Dessy, who had picked up a lot of the phrases of American football, if not much real understanding of it.

"Well, I can't imagine three more delightful children to have, all of a sudden," smiled Mrs Bantam.

The next morning, armed with the list of names that Janice had printed out, the three of them went to

Lisbeg graveyard. It was a cloudy day, and the tombstones looked forlorn and neglected. They stood at the gate and surveyed the gloomy scene. The wind ruffled the wild grass, and sighed in the trees like a forlorn cry of sadness from a departed spirit.

"Look over there," said Brendan, pointing to a grave on the left not far from the gateway. There was a carved angel on the top of the tombstone, and fresh chips of granite covered the flat grave. There was a round metal bowl too, with flowers in it.

"It looks as if another family has found a grave," said Molly. "Séamus has been active while we've been away in California." They went across to the grave, and she knelt down beside it. *In loving memory of Paul Brandt,*" she read.

Brendan took out a magnifying glass and peered at the name. "Yes, that's definitely been altered," he said, scraping the letters with his fingernail. "I can see what Séamus has done. The original name was *Brady*. He's squeezed in an *n* and altered the *y* at the end to a *t*. When you scratch away the dust you can see the new chiselling."

Molly looked at her list. "Here it is," she said. "*Brady*. It's one of the ones with a little star next to it."

Brendan got out his Polaroid camera and focussed it on the name. "I wish we had those lights from the movie studio, they would show it up really well," he said, as he clicked the shutter.

"Well, the Great Electrician in the Sky has come to help you out," said Dessy, as the sun came out from behind a cloud and shone down on the graves.

"Yes," said Brendan, "that shows up the hollowed-out letters much better." He clicked the shutter again.

Dessy looked up at the sky and said, "Thanks!"

"Let's get to work fast, while the sun stays out," said Brendan. "What are the other starred names?"

"Well, we know about the Darlys, for a start," said Molly. They moved across to the far side of the graveyard where Séamus had changed the *Daly* tombstone to *Darly*. Brendan focussed, and clicked the shutter.

"Where next?" he said.

"It's hard to know where to look," said Molly. "Why don't we all take a few names, and split up, and look at different graves?"

Brendan went over to the corner of the graveyard where Sailor Jack's tombstone was. He stared at it. He still had no clue about the code it was supposed to contain, the code that would lead them to the pirate's treasure. He shivered, remembering the strange sound like laughter which they had heard here. He examined the inscription again. This one definitely looked as if the lettering was all old, and hadn't been tampered with. After his fright the other day, Séamus might be too scared to mess with it.

Brendan began looking at the graves nearby.

Dessy was not far away, examining the graves near the side wall. Molly was in the middle of the graveyard, looking at a huge marble stone with a Celtic cross on top. On the front face of the marble was carved in big capital letters the one name, *SULLIVAN*. Underneath there were several names and dates. This must be a family vault.

She heard voices. Thinking it was Brendan and Dessy talking, she looked across to their side of the graveyard. But they were each peering at separate graves, away from each other.

In alarm, Molly glanced up towards the gateway. She could see a Land-Rover parked there. Séamus Gallagher was inside, talking to someone else.

She took out her tin whistle and made a bird-like sound on it. It was a signal. Brendan and Dessy both turned towards her, and she pointed up towards the gate. They could see Séamus getting out and coming towards the entrance. And with him was his daughter Dervla. So the famous "Doctor Galvin" had surfaced again after all.

Brendan was near the back wall of the graveyard and quickly jumped over it to hide in the bushes where they had hidden before. Dessy was just by the side wall, and Molly saw him dive head first over it, in amongst the trees.

There was no time for Molly to run across to the wall without being seen. She would have to stay where she was. She ducked down behind the large marble tombstone and crouched there.

She could hear the voices of Séamus and his daughter as they came into the graveyard. They were arguing.

"You shouldn't be out here!" said Séamus. "It's not safe. Someone might see you."

"I can't stay cooped up in that grotty pub all the time," said Dervla. "Besides, who's going to come to this god-forsaken place, except you and those fools you bring to look at their family graves?"

"But if people know you're back, they'll begin to ask questions again. Then they'll start suspecting I'm up to something, too."

"I wouldn't have had to come back at all, if you hadn't messed things up and sent those dreadful children sniffing around!"

"I didn't send them!" growled Séamus. "They're friends of that wretched Bantam boy. They must have gone to see him."

"I don't care how they came to be there, but they're on to us. They know too much. It's all your fault for bungling it."

"I didn't bungle it, it was you!"

By now the quarrelling pair had reached the tomb where Molly was hiding, and stopped just the other side of the big stone that hid her. She looked around, but there was nowhere to run. Luckily they decided to sit down on the raised stone that bordered the grave.

"Anyway," said Dervla, "it looks as if we may have to get out of the fake grave business while the going is good."

"But what about the money?" wailed Séamus.

"We'll make just as much from the property scam. I already made a start by telling those Darly people about the house they want to make into a heritage centre. They even bought the idea of you running it." She burst out laughing.

"It's not that far-fetched." Séamus was offended.

"What?" sneered Dervla. "Dad, you wouldn't know what heritage was if it came up and danced a jig for you."

Séamus grunted, and sat there sulking.

"We'll have to make this Mrs Morgan you're seeing the last of the ancestor-tracers," said Dervla. "After that, I'll go back and start finding likely buyers for fake properties instead."

"If only we could find that treasure of Sailor Jack's, we could retire for good," said Séamus.

"Pie in the sky, Dad," said Dervla. "You don't believe all that waffle, do you? If there ever was any treasure, it'll be long gone by now."

"If only we could crack that code," said Séamus.

"There's no code."

"There is, if only we knew what it was."

"Some people will believe anything. Come on then, show me. Perhaps I'll be able to work it out!" Dervla was sarcastic.

"It's all right, I have it written down, we don't need to go and look at it."

Dervla laughed. "Dad, I think you're scared!"

"Me? Of course I'm not. Me, scared of Sailor

Jack?" Séamus gave a hollow laugh which Molly thought sounded totally unconvincing.

"All right, come on then!" said Dervla. She got up from the stone. Molly realised that when they went that way they would pass behind the tombstone and her hiding-place. She looked around desperately.

Suddenly, from over in the direction of Sailor Jack's grave, there was a noise that sounded like a high-pitched, crazy laugh.

"What was that?" said Séamus, his voice shaking.

"I don't know, but I'm going to find out," said Dervla. "It's someone spying on us and playing tricks. Quick, come on!"

"I don't think. . ." said Séamus faintly.

"Oh, come on!" shouted Dervla, and she ran across the graveyard, followed stumblingly by Séamus. Molly stayed quite still. Fortunately they had been looking across to the corner of the graveyard and had set off so quickly they hadn't seen her. But now Molly was afraid they would find Brendan, hidden behind the wall beyond Sailor Jack's grave. It was brave of him to distract their attention, when he realised they were about to find Molly.

Molly crept round the other side of the tombstone to keep herself hidden, and peered round it to watch. She saw Dervla and Séamus stop at Sailor Jack's grave.

"You see," said Séamus, "there's nothing. Let's get back, there's no one here."

"Then who made that noise?" snapped Dervla.

Séamus was silent. "Oh no!" Dervla went on, "don't tell me you think it was some kind of ghost? Dad, you really are the limit! There's someone hiding round here, believe me. Over here, perhaps."

Molly watched in alarm as Dervla looked over the wall into the bushes where Brendan was hiding. Then she began to clamber over the wall.

"Who's there?" she called, landing on the far side of the wall. She picked up a tree branch and began beating at the bushes with it. Molly thought it could only be a few moments before Brendan was discovered. But to her surprise, after several minutes of pushing through the bushes and beating about, Dervla emerged.

"They've gone," she said. Molly was relieved. She wondered where Brendan had gone to hide, after he had done the laugh.

"Let's get out of here," said Séamus, beginning to move towards the gate. Dervla began to follow, but then stopped and said, "Wait!" She was looking back at the tombstone with Sailor Jack's epitaph.

Reluctantly, Séamus stopped and said, "What is it now?"

"The name on the inscription," said Dervla. "It's *Jack Moran.* And you're looking for a grave to show Mrs Morgan. What could be easier? All you have to do is carve a *g* in the middle there. Yes, Sailor Jack's is the grave you can alter. You can do it tonight!"

Molly saw Séamus go rather pale. He gazed at the tombstone glumly, then turned and hurried away towards the gate.

CHAPTER ELEVEN

Deals and Double-crosses

Molly lay low, peering around the grave until she saw Séamus and Dervla go through the gateway and get into the Land-Rover and drive away. She took out her tin whistle and gave the bird signal. Then for fun she started to play a reel.

Dessy's head popped up over the wall from the woods where he had disappeared earlier. He grinned and waved, and climbed back over the wall. He came towards Molly, clapping his hands and doing some dance steps. Molly stopped playing when he reached her.

"Where's Brendan?" she asked. "I thought Dervla was going to find him. They'd have found *me* if he hadn't given that laugh to distract their attention."

Dessy called, "Brendan, you can come out now."

A voice called back, "OK, down I come!" From high in one of the trees in the wood behind the bushes, came two dangling legs. The legs kicked till they found a branch, and then Brendan appeared, climbing down the tree. He scrambled over the wall and came across the graveyard to join them.

Molly blew a triumphant blast on her whistle to welcome him. Then she said, "Thanks, Brendan, they would have spotted me if it hadn't been for you."

"I saw them get up and start moving near where you were, so I thought I'd hurry them up," said Brendan.

"I was sure they'd find you in the bushes," said Molly.

"I wasn't there. I shinned up the tree straight away. It was just as well I did. Dervla was whacking those bushes so hard she would have beaten me to a pulp."

Molly told them what she had overheard from her hiding-place.

"So it looks like the "Mrs Morgan" tracing will be our last chance to catch them red-handed," said Brendan.

"He'll be here tonight to carve the fake name," said Dessy, "and we'll be here too. We can even have a bit of fun scaring him with a few Sailor Jack noises. How about this?" He began singing,

"Fifteen men on a dead man's chest,
Yo-ho-ho and a bottle of rum!"

"That doesn't sound very ghostly to me," said Brendan.

"Just drinky!" said Molly. "We'll leave the ghostly noises to Brendan. He's becoming an expert."

"Thanks," said Brendan. Then he added thoughtfully, "It's an odd thing, but when I was doing that laugh, I almost thought another voice was laughing with me. And when I stopped, I still seemed to hear a sound rustling in the trees. It was like a voice just saying one word . . . *Num* . . . *Num* . . . *Num* . . . "

"Just the wind in the leaves, I expect," said Molly uneasily. She shivered.

Brendan said, "It sounded so real, but I don't know whether it was in the air or in my own head. It felt as if it was some kind of a message."

"A message? Who from?" said Dessy. They all looked down at the grave of Sailor Jack. There was silence. Then a crow cawed, up in one of the trees. The sound broke the spell.

"It's time we got back," said Molly nervously.

They moved away towards the gate in silence. Brendan glanced back once or twice at the tomb of Sailor Jack in the far corner. Was it possible that it was the pirate's voice he had heard, calling across the gulf between the dead and the living? But the tomb looked as peaceful and undisturbed as an ancient rock. Brendan hoped it would remain so tonight, when they came to see Séamus tampering with it.

"OK, guys, into the huddle! Now, quarterback, you block him out and I'll lateral to you, and you go long . . . "

The three of them were crouched in a huddle on the lawn terrace at the end of the hotel garden. They were wearing their football helmets and Dessy, as self-styled Captain of the Ballygandon Bears team, was giving them the instructions for play. On the balcony of the terrace six feet above them sat Mrs Bantam, with a table laid ready for tea, waiting for Séamus Gallagher.

The idea was that in her role as Mrs Morgan, she would be watching her three "children" practising American football. Dessy had decided that they must take their roles seriously, and was mustering all the terms he could think of to instruct his team.

"I don't understand a word you're saying, Dessy," said Brendan.

"Why can't we just kick the ball around like we usually do?" said Molly, "without all this stuff about blocking out and going long?"

"Because it wouldn't look like the real thing," said Dessy. "We've got to fool Séamus."

"Séamus wouldn't know what we were playing," said Molly.

"I think he's coming," called Mrs Bantam from the balcony above.

"Right, let's play!" cried Dessy.

"OK," said Brendan, "but when they start talking properly, we'll drift in gradually so that we're under the balcony and can hear what they say, while pretending to go on playing."

"Good afternoon, Mrs Morgan, how delightful to see you," they heard Séamus say in his attempt at a posh voice, as he approached across the upper lawn. Then they heard a bark.

"It sounds as if he's brought that horrible dog with him," said Dessy.

"Good afternoon, Mr Gallagher," said Mrs Bantam, "do come and sit down and we'll have some tea."

"Thank you," said Séamus. "Sit, Lonnigan, good boy!"

Seeing Séamus glance curiously over the balcony at the helmetted figures, Mrs Bantam said, "Those are my children . . . er . . . Hank, Bobby and Mary Lou. They're mad about football."

Séamus raised his hand in greeting and the three of them waved back and shouted, "Hi!"

Then Dessy yelled, "OK, team, GO-GO-GO!" They went rushing down the lawn, passing the ball from hand to hand. Suddenly there was a yelp, and into the middle of the game bounded Lonnigan, leaping up and down, yapping and trying to catch the ball. Dessy clutched it to his chest, and

Lonnigan jumped on to him, nearly pushing him over.

"Lonnigan! Come here, boy! Lonnigan!" Séamus shouted, leaning over the balcony.

"Get off, you slobbering oaf!" said Dessy.

Séamus grabbed one of the sandwiches from the tea-table and held it out. "Lonnigan, look! Eaties!"

The dog left Dessy and rushed back up the steps on to the terrace. He began wolfing down the sandwich. Séamus gave him another, saying, "These will keep him quiet."

"I hope there will be some left for *us*," said Mrs Bantam coldly. "Now, have you any news for me?"

"I certainly have," said Séamus, opening his brief-case and taking out some papers.

The footballers went into a huddle just under the balcony, pretending to talk about tactics, so that they could listen to the conversation.

"I have researched our comprehensive list of family names and graves," Séamus was saying, "and I have discovered that the name Morgan does indeed feature there, and according to the details you gave me, it looks as if it is your own original family."

"Well, I am just delighted," said Mrs Bantam. "Somehow, I felt sure you'd trace it."

"What's more," said Séamus, "according to our records, there is a Morgan grave in this area, not far away from here, in the graveyard of Lisbeg."

"Oh, I'm so excited!" said Mrs Bantam. "Can we go and see it right away?"

Brendan smiled at the others under his helmet. He wondered what Séamus would do.

"Er . . . not today, that wouldn't be . . . er . . . suitable," Séamus bumbled. "You see, I need to make an advance examination of Lisbeg, and find the exact location of this particular grave . . ."

"Tomorrow, then?"

"Certainly, it will be ready . . . I mean it will be found by tomorrow."

"Shall we say eleven o'clock?'"

"That will be fine, Mrs Morgan," Séamus said. "I'll collect you here at the hotel. And in due course we shall also provide you with a complete family tree and scroll, and a history of the Morgan family."

"Wonderful, just wonderful!" Mrs Bantam exclaimed. "Till tomorrow then." She got up to say goodbye, but Séamus stayed where he was, nervously fingering his brief-case. Lonnigan, full of sandwiches, was lying asleep on the grass.

"There was just one other matter . . ." said Séamus.

"Yes?" asked Mrs Bantam pleasantly.

In the huddle below the balcony, Molly whispered, "The money!" The others grinned.

Molly was right. Séamus said, "You'll understand that there is considerable expense involved in the kind of research we do, and I was wondering if . . ."

"Oh, of course!" said Mrs Bantam. "How

thoughtless of me. Naturally you must have your fee. Now, what figure had you in mind?"

"Shall we say a thousand as an advance, and the same again when we have completed the graveyard visit?"

The trio on the lower terrace looked at each other wide-eyed. This was even more than the figures set out in the brochure they had seen.

Mrs Bantam said pleasantly, "That sounds very reasonable. Would you like it in cash straight away?"

Séamus could hardly believe his good fortune. "Well, yes, that would be excellent," he said.

Brendan looked at the others. They were as worried as he was. They knew that if Mrs Bantam handed over any cash to Séamus, she would never see it again.

They listened glumly as they heard her say, "I have it here in my bag. You don't mind taking it in US dollars, I suppose?"

"Of course not, thank you."

"I don't know just what the exchange rate is right now, but let's call it seventeen hundred dollars. We can sort it out more precisely later. Now, I have the notes here . . . fifty, one hundred, one hundred and fifty . . . "

The footballers looked dismayed as they heard the figures. When Mrs Bantam had finished and Séamus had pocketed the money, they said goodbye and Séamus went away across the lawn, leading the well-fed Lonnigan.

"I bet Séamus is grinning from ear to ear," said Dessy.

"What could Mrs Bantam be thinking of, handing out all that cash?" Molly wondered.

"Hi there!" Mrs Bantam was leaning over the balcony. "Would the team like to join me for a tea-break? The dog has left us a few sandwiches!"

When they were seated at the table, Brendan was about to take off his helmet, when Dessy said, "Hey, we'd better stay in disguise. You never know, Séamus might come back, or someone else might recognise us."

"OK," said Brendan reluctantly. It wasn't easy feeding yourself sandwiches and cakes through the face-guards of the helmets, but they managed it somehow.

"Well, what did you think of my performance?" asked Mrs Bantam.

"It was wonderful," said Molly, and the others agreed.

"Is anything wrong? You look a bit worried."

"Well, it's just that . . . all that money . . ." said Molly.

Mrs Bantam laughed. "Oh, it wasn't real money! I got it from my friends at the studio. It's the fake money they use in the movies. It looks just like the real thing, doesn't it?" She took some notes from her bag and showed them around.

"I guess that will fool Séamus," said Brendan, "it would certainly fool me."

"He's greedy, all right," said Molly, relieved.

She soon discovered he was even greedier than they thought. She went into the hotel to go to the Rest Room, as she now liked to call it, and in the hallway she heard the familiar voice of Séamus. She dodged behind a pillar, and spotted him with Lonnigan in a phone booth at the side of the hall. She dashed across and stood behind the booth where Séamus was speaking. He must be talking to Dervla.

"It all went very well," he was saying. "Everything's on course for tomorrow. What did you say? Oh, the money. No, I haven't got any yet, but she'll give it all to us tomorrow when she's seen the Morgan grave . . ."

Molly smiled to herself. So Séamus was planning to double-cross his own daughter, and keep the money without telling her about it. He must think himself very clever. And he didn't know that the wad of bank-notes was worth absolutely nothing!

It was growing dark as they approached Lisbeg in Locky's car. Molly's parents had agreed that he could take them on an outing to the cinema. When asked what the film was called, Locky had said cheerfully, "I think it's called . . . *The Mystery Graves*."

In the car Locky said, "Well, it's not that far from the truth. It's just that the 'Mystery Graves' are real instead of on film." They went past the gateway and on down the winding road till they were out of sight of the graveyard. Locky parked the car in a lane and they walked back.

They made their way between the tombstones. The place was even more gloomy and melancholy in the dusk. There were clouds in the sky, hiding the moon which occasionally peered out from behind them and shone unearthly beams of pale light down on the scene.

They came to Sailor Jack's grave and gazed at it for a while. Once more Brendan puzzled about the inscription. What secret did it hide? And were there other secrets hidden in the grave itself, horrible secrets lurking, ready to emerge if anyone tried to tamper with the ancient grave?

Brendan shivered as he remembered the strange voice he had heard in his head . . . *"Num . . . Num . . . Num . . . "*

Just then they heard a real sound – the distant rumble of a vehicle approaching. It must be Séamus's Land-Rover.

"We must take cover," said Dessy. He climbed over the wall behind the grave. Then Brendan and Molly helped Locky to get up on to the wall, and Dessy helped him down on the other side.

Soon all four of them were well hidden in the bushes, with a perfect view of the graveyard and Sailor Jack's grave nearby. Up on the road they saw the lights of the Land-Rover approach, then stop and go out. Brendan clutched his camera and Molly and Dessy had flashlights ready for the big moment when they would get the final evidence of Séamus's crimes.

They watched the dark figure and the beam of a torch appear at the gate, and slowly come towards them across the graveyard.

CHAPTER TWELVE

The Ghost Walks

As Locky and the three Ballygandon Private Eyes watched from their hiding-place, Séamus picked his way carefully over the bumpy, grass-covered graveyard. Occasionally he stumbled over a half-hidden gravestone, and they heard him curse. He was carrying a hold-all. There was no sign of the dog Lonnigan.

Séamus stopped a short distance away from Sailor Jack's grave, and gazed at it. They could hear him breathing heavily. Brendan realised it wasn't just because Séamus had been walking – he was scared. They watched him standing there, trying to summon up the courage to approach the grave.

Then they heard him growl, "I won't let you get the better of *me*, you miserable old mariner! I'm going to make a lot of money out of you. I wonder how you'll like your new name?" Séamus gave a bitter laugh, and strode to the side of the grave.

He put his torch down, propped on a stone, so

that it shone on the inscription. Then he knelt down in front of the tombstone, on the grave itself. He rummaged in his hold-all and brought out a chisel and a mallet. To keep his spirits up, he began singing to himself. It was the very song that Dessy had suggested:

Fifteen men on a dead man's chest,
Yo-ho-ho, and a bottle of rum . . .

Séamus sang in a gruff, tuneless voice, the song punctuated by the tapping of the chisel against the stone.

Brendan whispered, "We need to get a picture of the front of the stone; from here at the back, we won't be able to show what he's doing."

Molly said, "OK, why don't you and Dessy creep round behind the wall and climb over the side wall into the graveyard so you're behind Séamus's back? I'll go the other way so that I'm behind him on the other side. Then our flashlights will catch him in a cross-beam, just as he finishes carving the name, and Brendan can run in and take the picture."

"What will be the signal to switch on?" Dessy asked.

"I'll make an owl-call on my tin whistle," said Molly. "When you hear that, it's on with the lights."

"Lights, camera, action!" said Dessy excitedly.

"Sssh!" said Brendan. They looked at Séamus. He had heard nothing. He was still singing tunelessly, and chipping away at the tombstone.

112

"Will you be OK on your own here, Grandpa?" asked Molly.

"Sure," said Locky, "graveyards don't bother me. I'll see you later. And good luck."

They crept away, treading warily. Once a twig cracked under Molly's foot, and Séamus looked round. Molly ducked down behind a tombstone. There was silence for a short while, though Molly felt the pounding of her heart must be loud enough to be heard all over the graveyard. But Séamus turned back to his carving and began singing again. It wouldn't be long now before he had finished the letter *g* and changed *Moran* to *Morgan*.

Soon they were in position, a good way behind Séamus. They saw him stop chiselling and pick up the torch, shining it closely on the inscription. Then they heard him grunt, "Rest in peace, Captain *Morgan!*" He gave a sneering laugh as he stared at the inscription.

It was time to take the picture. Molly took out her tin whistle and blew an owl-hoot on it, then another. Then she switched on her flashlight and pointed it at the grave. On the other side of the graveyard, Dessy's flashlight went on. Brendan clicked his camera, then moved forward for a closer shot, as Séamus turned in alarm.

"What's going on?" he yelled.

Then with a cry he turned back again to look at the tombstone and the wall behind it. Molly gasped, and she and Brendan and Dessy all stood dead still, as if they'd been turned to stone.

There was a figure standing on the wall. At first Molly was annoyed. "Why has Grandpa Locky decided to come out of hiding?" she thought. "He could mess up everything."

Then she felt the hair on her head begin to prickle with fear. She stared, wide-eyed, as the figure that had looked like Locky seemed to glow with an unearthly light and change its appearance. Now, instead of Locky, Molly saw standing there on the wall, swaying a little, a man in a tattered tunic with gold buttons, wearing breeches and long boots. On his head was a mariner's cap and beneath it his bearded face, streaked with blood, seemed to be contorted with rage.

The figure lifted its right hand and pointed at Séamus. A kind of growling groan came from its lips, and seemed to echo all around the graveyard. An icy wind blew through the tombstones, making the long grass rustle and wave.

As the figure went on pointing its bony hand at him, Séamus sank to his knees with his hands stretched out, pleading. "No, Sailor Jack, no!" he wailed, "don't hurt me. Don't hurt me. I didn't mean it! No, please, no!" He was gibbering with fright and began weeping and moaning as he clasped his hands together and stared transfixed at the apparition.

Suddenly the groans coming from the figure changed to a mad, shrieking laugh which seemed to dart among the tombstones and whistle through the trees. The laugh was repeated again and again.

As they watched, the phantom bent down and stepped off the wall. Slowly it began to approach Séamus, its hands stretched out as though it was planning to seize him by the throat.

Séamus let out a high-pitched scream, and both Molly and Dessy dropped their flashlights in fright. All three of them stood rooted to the spot in terror, feeling an icy chill come over their limbs.

The phantom had its own luminous glow as it came forward, seeming to glide and float over the ground towards its own grave. The laughter got louder and more maniacal as the apparition got nearer to Séamus. He seemed to be transfixed, like a rabbit in the headlights of a car. But then, as the bony hands reached out to seize him, he turned to run. Screaming and flailing his arms, he staggered and stumbled towards the gateway, crashing into tombstones and falling down and scrambling up again.

Now and then he looked back, to see the figure coming slowly after him. When he reached the gate he grabbed the gatepost and held on to it, gasping for breath. He looked back towards the figure.

Molly and the others still stood watching in terror. Then suddenly the apparition's laugh changed to a choking gasp, and its hands went to its own throat. It cried out as if it was strangling, and with a final cry it crumpled and collapsed on the ground and lay perfectly still. The weird glowing light faded gradually out, and only a dark huddled shape lay on the ground.

Séamus didn't wait to see any more. He decided to escape while he could. He clambered into the Land-Rover and started the engine. The vehicle moved away at reckless speed, weaving erratically down the road.

There was an eerie silence in the graveyard. None of them felt able to move. It was as if a spell had been cast over them. Then, in the distance, a dog barked. With a jerk, Molly felt the use of her limbs come back. She picked up the flashlight and shone it towards Brendan and Dessy. They too had come out of the trance they had seemed to be in.

"Are you OK, Molly?" Brendan called.

"Yes, fine. Are you?"

"Sure, we're fine now," said Dessy.

Molly called out towards the far corner of the graveyard, "Grandpa, are you all right?" There was no reply.

Brendan called, "Grandpa?" Again there was no answer.

They all rushed over to the wall behind Sailor Jack's grave, and clambered over it. They shone their flashlights into the bushes and began pulling the branches aside. The spot where Locky had been hiding was completely empty. They searched around in the bushes, flashing their lights and calling, "Grandpa! Grandpa!" But there was no sign of Locky.

Brendan stopped and said, "He's not here. He's disappeared."

"He can't have done," said Molly.

Dessy said nervously, "You don't suppose the . . . the thing . . . it . . . whatever it was . . . could have done him in?"

"Of course not," said Brendan, sounding far from sure.

"But he'd still be here," said Molly, "even if . . ." She gulped. She couldn't bring herself to say what might have happened. This was a nightmare. Were they all going crazy and seeing visions of horror? Had Locky gone mad too and run off into the woods in terror? She wished the night was over, or had never begun.

"Listen!" said Brendan. They were all silent. Then they heard from up in the graveyard a faint moaning sound. They looked at each other in fear.

"What is it?" asked Dessy. But they knew they had to go towards the sound to find out. They climbed back over the wall and shone their flashlights up the graveyard. The tombstones stood like watchful creatures waiting. Waiting for what?

There was another moan. As they got nearer, they realised that it came from the place where the apparition had stopped and collapsed. Brendan had expected to find that it had faded away or crumbled to dust, but as they reached the spot, they saw what looked like a real body huddled on the ground.

There was another moan, and they shone their flashlights full on the figure. The body sat up, and they saw the face blinking in the bright light. It was Locky.

With cries of "Grandpa! Grandpa!" they rushed over to him. Molly hugged him and said with a sob in her voice, "Grandpa, you're safe! Are you all right? We were so scared."

"*You* were scared?" he said. "Well, I've never been more frightened in my life. What happened?"

"Didn't you see it?" asked Brendan.

"See what?"

"The thing . . . the ghost . . . Sailor Jack. It came after Séamus, right up to where you are now, and then collapsed." Brendan knelt down and he and Dessy helped Locky up and sat him down on the wall of a raised grave.

"All I can remember," said Locky, "is watching Séamus chiselling away at the tombstone, then just being able to see you in the darkness, creeping across the graveyard. I wanted to be in at the finish, so I quietly climbed on to the wall. Then suddenly your lights went on, and the weirdest feeling came over me."

"What sort of feeling?" Molly asked.

"As if I was in the grip of some power. Almost as if I had no will of my own any more. I was like a puppet with someone else inside, moving me about. It was terrifying. I remember my hand being raised, and walking towards Sailor Jack's grave, and Séamus kneeling there. Then I heard him wailing and screaming, but I don't remember anything after that. It's all a hazy blur. Then I must have passed out. When I came to, I was lying here, with a bad headache."

They told him again about the vision that seemed

to be the ghost of Sailor Jack, and how they had seen him standing on the wall, and raising his finger just as Locky said *he* had done, then stepping down from the wall and moving towards Séamus, again just as Locky remembered himself doing. And the apparition had ended up right here in the middle of the graveyard, just where they had found Locky.

They all looked at one another, puzzling. Then Locky said with a note of terror in his voice, "I think you saw *me*."

"*You?*" said Molly. "But what we saw, or what *I* saw, was this ghastly figure that looked like Sailor Jack, with blood on his face, groaning and laughing."

Brendan and Dessy said that was exactly what *they* had seen too.

"I can't explain it," said Locky, "but it seems to me that somehow I was possessed. The spirit of Sailor Jack saw a chance to take charge of a real body and come after the man who was messing with his grave. I just happened to be in the right place at the right time . . . the right place for *him*, that is!"

"Oh, I'm so glad you're all right, Grandpa," said Molly, hugging Locky again. "He could have killed you."

"It was Séamus he wanted to kill," said Locky. "He might have done it, too, using *my* body." He looked down at his own hands, the hands that had been stretched out ready to strangle the man who

119

had violated the grave. They looked across at the tomb of Sailor Jack. It seemed to glow with an unearthly light. The faint sound of laughter echoed again around the graveyard, laughter that was full of menace.

"Let's get out of here," said Locky. They all went stumbling through the grass towards the gateway, Brendan and Dessy on each side of Locky, helping him along.

When they reached the gate they looked back at Sailor Jack's grave. Gradually the light from it seemed to fade, and at the same time the laughter died down into silence.

The graveyard seemed still and serene now, with no hint of any ghostly presence. But they felt sure it was still there, lurking . . . and waiting.

CHAPTER THIRTEEN

Tombstone Puzzles

Locky drove very slowly and nervously back to Ballygandon. In the front seat beside him, Molly peered into the darkness beyond the headlights' beams, half-expecting to see the ghastly figure of Sailor Jack looming up in front of them.

Just as they were approaching the village, Brendan said, "Hey, I've just thought of something."

"Careful," said Dessy, "you'll damage your brain if you go on using it so hard."

"It's serious," said Brendan. "We missed a chance. When Séamus rushed away up the graveyard, he left his hold-all and tools behind by Sailor Jack's grave. We should have brought them with us. They would have been great evidence."

"Well, we can't go back now," said Locky.

"But Séamus might go back tonight and get them," said Brendan.

"We'll have to chance that," said Locky, "but my guess is he'll be too scared to go back in the dark in case the ghost comes after him again. I'll take you there first thing in the morning, while the rest of you talk to the Guards and show them the photographs. Then you can bring them to meet us at the graveyard, and we can all wait for Séamus and Mrs Bantam, and be ready to spring the trap!"

"Maybe Séamus will be too scared after tonight even to turn up tomorrow," said Dessy.

"Oh, he'll be there, I'm sure," said Molly. "He wants the rest of the money for a start, and anyway Dervla will make sure he goes through with it."

Next morning early, Brendan and his grandfather were rattling along in Locky's ancient car. "I'm not an early bird," Locky grumbled, "I don't know why we need to be out and about at the crack of dawn."

"It's nine o'clock, Grandpa!" said Brendan.

"That's what I mean, the crack of dawn," said Locky. "Molly's mother was surprised enough that we're all going on an outing so early."

"Well, we said we're meeting Billy's mother later on, which is true," said Brendan. "I just hope we're in time to find that hold-all with Séamus's tools in it. It's vital evidence."

Locky grunted.

"Grandpa," Brendan went on, "you don't mind going back to the graveyard, do you? I mean, you're not afraid or anything?"

"Afraid? Of course not," said Locky gruffly. "Are you?"

"No." But neither of them sounded convincing.

122

"What kind of time do you call this?" said the local guard, Emma Delaney, when she saw Molly and Dessy standing on the doorstep of her house in Ballygandon at nine o'clock in the morning.

"I'm sorry," said Molly, "but it's urgent."

"Well, this is my day off," said Emma, "can't you contact the Garda station in town about it?"

"It's big stuff that's going down here," said Dessy, remembering some slang he'd heard in a movie. "A chance to hit the big time, crime-wise."

"I don't know what you're talking about," said Emma, "but I suppose you'd better come in for a minute."

They told Emma what they had discovered about Tree Tracers, and about their investigations in California and in the local graveyard, and their plans to catch Séamus.

They showed her the photographs Brendan had taken of the graves that had been tampered with. There was even one that he had shot last night. It was a bit blurred, but you could definitely see a figure standing on a grave with something in his hand.

"That does look a bit like Séamus Gallagher all right," said Emma, "but it doesn't show he's doing anything wrong." Then she smiled and said, "I don't suppose he was best pleased by a sudden flash photograph, whatever he was up to. I wonder he didn't beat you up, he's got quite a temper."

Molly was about to tell Emma the reason Séamus didn't do anything to them, but she decided against making a full description of the ghostly appearance of Sailor Jack. Emma would think they were making the whole thing up.

"We just want you to come and see the graves he's been messing around with," said Molly, "and then we can hide when he turns up with Mrs Bantam, and catch him red-handed." She just hoped that Séamus *would* turn up. She was fairly sure that the lure of money would conquer his fears, in the end.

Emma Delaney didn't think her superiors in the Guards would rate the story and the photographs as anything more than some kind of fantasy the children were making up. But reluctantly she agreed to take them to the graveyard, just to have a look.

Locky parked his car out of sight down the lane, and he and Brendan walked to the graveyard. Birds were singing, and it was hard to imagine the scary events that had happened here last night. As soon as they reached the gate, Brendan ran across the graveyard. When he reached Sailor Jack's tombstone in the corner, he saw the new name, *Morgan*, on the inscription. But there was no sign of the hold-all.

Locky arrived to find Brendan scrabbling round in the earth and the loose stones. "It's gone!" he said.

"He must have snatched it up and taken it with him," said Locky.

"No," said Brendan, "I'm sure he wasn't carrying it when he ran off."

"Then he must have come back for it last night, or very early this morning."

"We should have come back last night ourselves," said Brendan dejectedly.

"Never mind." Locky tried to cheer his grandson up. "We've still got your splendid photographs, and Molly and Dessy will be here soon with the Guards to see the graves themselves. Why don't you take some more pictures of Sailor Jack's grave now that we can see the way Séamus has changed it, in the daylight?"

Brendan was glad of the distraction while they waited for the others. He began to take close-up pictures of the inscription. As he did so, he thought he heard that sound again: the voice murmuring, *"Num . . . Num . . . Num . . ."* Was it just in his head, he wondered, or was someone trying to tell him something?

The sound at the end seemed to be drawn-out, as if the voice was starting a word and trying to finish it. *"Num . . . Num . . ."*

"That's it!" thought Brendan suddenly. It *was* only part of a word, the full word was *Number*! The voice was trying to say the word *Number*, or maybe *Numbers*. It was telling him where to look for the clue to the code: in the numbers on the inscription which gave Sailor Jack's date of birth.

Brendan put away his camera and got out his

notebook. He must start straight away. Now he had narrowed it down, but he still had to crack the code to find out what the numbers meant. Just then he heard Locky's voice from up by the gateway calling, "Here come the Guards!"

Brendan went across to the gate. He was disappointed to see that it was only an ordinary car, and not a Garda car with a proper sign that could flash and maybe even sound a siren when they took Séamus Gallagher away. That would have been really dramatic.

When the car was parked out of sight down the lane, Emma Delaney came back towards the gateway with Molly and Dessy. Brendan was sorry to see that the only Guard was Emma Delaney, and she wasn't in uniform.

When she came up to Locky and Brendan, Emma explained that she was only doing this as a favour, just in case there was anything in it. She seemed surprised to see Locky there.

"Mr Loughlin, isn't it? I've seen you in the village now and then. Aren't you Molly's grandfather?"

"That's right," said Locky, "and Brendan's. A bright pair of kids. So is their friend Dessy here. They're great detectives!"

"Well, we'll see about that," said Emma. "Now let's have a look at these graves you say Séamus Gallagher has been messing about with."

"This way," said Molly, leading Emma first

towards the *Darly* grave. The others followed, and they all stood round the grave.

"There!" said Brendan.

Emma bent down and looked at the inscription. "What's wrong with it?" she asked.

Brendan leaned forward and said, "You see, the name has been changed from . . ." His voice tailed away and he felt himself go cold. The name on the inscription was *Daly*. "I can't believe it!" he exclaimed.

"What's wrong?" said Molly. She and Dessy came closer to look at it too.

"But it *was* changed, it *was*!" cried Dessy. "We saw it, he put in an extra *r*. " He went close to the stone and began to scrape with his finger. But the carved *r* had been filled in with some kind of hard cement, and then dusted over so you couldn't tell it had ever been there.

They all stared at the tombstone in amazement.

"He must have come and changed it back," said Molly. "Last night, or early today."

"Come over here," said Brendan, setting out for the place where the *Brady* grave was, the one Séamus had changed to *Brandt*. They followed him, but it was just as he feared. The inscription had been changed back to *Brady*.

"Listen," said Emma, "I know this is my day off, but there is an offence called *Wasting Police Time*!"

"I'm sure they're telling the truth, Emma," said Locky. But visits to some of the other graves Séamus had altered didn't back him up.

"Look at the photographs," said Brendan. "They show what the graves were like."

"You can do a lot of tricks with photographs," said Emma.

"Wait, we haven't looked at Sailor Jack's grave yet," said Brendan. "That hasn't been altered back."

He led the way across to the corner of the graveyard and pointed at the inscription triumphantly. Emma went forward and examined it.

"You're right," she said, "this one has certainly had something done to it. An extra *g* has been squeezed in, to make *Moran* into *Morgan*. But it's going to be hard to prove Séamus Gallagher did it."

"Not if you wait a little while, and watch him trying to con Mrs Bantam," said Molly.

Emma Delaney wasn't convinced, but she agreed to stay. They concealed themselves in the bushes at the back of the wall behind Sailor Jack's grave.

"We've been lurking here so often we could almost set up camp," said Brendan. As they waited, he scribbled in his notebook, trying to make sense of the coded numbers from the inscription.

"I think I can hear the Land-Rover," said Molly.

"OK," said Dessy, "time for me to take the stage." To the surprise of the others, he produced his football helmet from the tote-bag he was carrying, put it on, and jumped over the wall.

"Dessy, what are you doing? You'll ruin everything!" Molly cried.

"It'll be good to have someone close to the action," said Dessy, "and Séamus thinks I'm one of Mrs Morgan's all-American children. Well, I'm off to join my Mom!"

"Dessy, come back here," cried Locky, but before they could stop him he was running up towards the gate.

They saw the Land-Rover pull up, and Séamus Gallagher help Mrs Bantam out. She was dressed in a smart check coat, with a pink silk scarf and a large blue straw hat. She had clearly decided to dress showily for her big performance.

They saw Dessy reach her and call out, "Hi, Mom!"

His "Mom" was clearly astonished to see him, but she recovered and gave him a pat on the head, saying, "Oh, hi there, er . . . Hank. I didn't expect to see you here."

"Neither did I," they heard Séamus growl.

"Dessy's such an *eejit*," said Brendan, "he'll ruin the whole thing if he's not careful."

"He'll probably start telling them a few graveyard jokes any minute," said Locky. Brendan thought it was all too likely.

They watched the three figures at the gate. Séamus seemed to be hesitating. He was pointing in the direction of Sailor Jack's grave, and muttering something to "Mrs Morgan". He must be suggesting that she go across and look at the grave on her own. He was too scared to approach it himself. No wonder, thought Molly, after what he had seen the night before.

Then she was startled to see another figure join them at the gateway, a woman wearing a headscarf and carrying a brief-case. She heard the woman say, "You *will* go to the grave yourself!"

"Please, no . . . " Séamus stuttered.

"Please, yes!" said the woman, pulling him by the hand. Now the hidden watchers recognised who she was. It was Séamus's daughter, Dervla.

"She's taking a risk coming out," said Brendan.

"It's my guess she had to, so as to make Séamus come. He is frightened of what might happen to him."

"Then who came and altered the graves back?" asked Locky.

"It could have been Dervla," said Molly, "during the night. She's probably as handy with a chisel as she is with a computer programme."

Emma Delaney said, "Dervla Gallagher! I knew that name rang a bell. She's wanted for questioning about all kinds of unsolved cases. It's all in the files at the Garda station. Now you've got me really interested."

Séamus led the way towards Sailor Jack's grave, looking shaky, with Dervla behind him, giving him the occasional push to urge him forward. "Mrs Morgan" followed and the helmetted Dessy brought up the rear.

From their hiding-place, the four onlookers observed the curious procession as it wound its way slowly between the tombstones towards them.

CHAPTER FOURTEEN

TREASURE HUNT

They reached Sailor Jack's grave, and stood in a group around it. Séamus kept gulping and biting his lip as he gazed at the tombstone, expecting at any moment that the grisly spectre of Sailor Jack would appear again.

"Well, there it is, Mrs Morgan," he said in a shaky voice, pointing at the inscription. "Your family grave."

"My, oh my!" cried Billy's mother, holding up her hands in delight. She stepped forward to take a closer look at the tombstone, then said, "Yes, there it is, Jack MORGAN, as large as life . . . well, not *life* exactly! Though in a way I can really feel his presence hovering around."

Séamus gave a faint groan, and shuddered. Dervla, standing beside him, jabbed him in the ribs with her elbow.

Billy's mother struck a dramatic pose, with one hand on her chest and the other stretched up into the air. In a ringing voice, as if she was performing a star part in a tragic play, she read out the inscription:

"Here lie the mortal remains of JACK MORGAN, king of the high seas.

I was born on the 7th day of the 1st month of the year 1829, at 5 o'clock in the morning.

My spirit will never die. Beware all who meddle with this noble grave. Torment shall be theirs. Rest in peace, Jack, as your enemies never will."

Hearing the words promising vengeance to meddlers, Séamus gave another groan, and received another jab in the ribs from Dervla. Dessy applauded, and Billy's mother stretched her hands out and bowed.

Then she said, "Imagine! Here he is, my very own ancestor. Jack Morgan, king of the high seas. Here I am, Jack, your Californian relation, who has travelled across those high seas to greet you."

The watchers in the bushes were startled to see Billy's mother fling herself forward and kneel on the grave, hugging the tombstone. Brendan said, "She's a bit over the top, isn't she?"

"She's an actress," whispered Molly. "I think she's doing a great job."

Suddenly they heard a rumbling sound, like distant thunder, except that it was close by. They all looked at one another. They saw Billy's mother stand up rather quickly from the grave.

"That's strange," she said, "I thought I felt the tombstone shake as I held it."

"You see," said Molly, "isn't that brilliant acting? Look at Séamus."

Séamus was standing there shivering, his eyes wide with terror. He was breathing rapidly.

"What's the matter?" asked Billy's mother.

"Nothing's the matter!" snapped Dervla. "Now that you have seen the grave, Mrs Morgan, perhaps we can conclude our arrangement. I have the family tree and the Morgan papers for you here." She held up the brief-case.

"But of course, Doctor . . . Galvin, is that the name?"

"That's right."

In the bushes, Emma Delaney looked enquiringly at Molly and Brendan. Molly whispered, "That's her fake name, in California."

Billy's mother produced her handbag, and said, "Well, I see no reason why we shouldn't settle up here and now, do you?"

"Excellent, excellent," said Séamus in a trembling voice.

From the handbag came a roll of bank-notes. Séamus took them in both hands. Dervla opened her brief-case and took out a large envelope and handed it over, saying, "Here are the papers and your family tree, Mrs Morgan."

"Thank you, Doctor Galvin, and thank *you*, Mr Gallagher." She struck a dramatic pose again. "Thanks to you, I have found the grave of my long-lost ancestor, JACK MORGAN!"

"OK, here we go," said Emma Delaney, preparing to come out of the bushes and over the wall.

But before she could move, there was another peal of thunder, which turned into a sound like a long-drawn-out howl of rage. At the same time, the tombstone began to shake, and the stones on and around the grave heaved and trembled. It was like an earthquake.

Everyone including the onlookers in the bushes froze in fright as they gazed on the scene. Billy's mother had her hands up to her mouth in a gesture of horror, but this time she wasn't acting.

Suddenly Séamus let out a scream and pointed at the grave, wailing, "He's there! He's there! I see him! Sailor Jack! He's coming after me!"

"Stop raving!" shouted Dervla, holding on to him and shaking him. But she sounded frightened herself.

"Please, Sailor Jack, don't stare at me like that!" Séamus cried. He was seeing the ghastly apparition, but this time it was appearing only to him. Séamus fell to his knees and howled, "I'll give it back, Sailor Jack, here, have it all!" He flung the rolled-up banknotes at the grave. They scattered into the air in the slight breeze, some of them falling on the heaving stones, others blowing about the graveyard.

At that moment the rumbling roar and the angry howls changed into the maniac laughter they had heard before. Séamus clutched his throat and called out, "No, no, no! Mercy! Mercy!" Then he fell full-length on the ground, shaking and crying.

All of a sudden, the sounds ceased, and the tombstone and the grave stopped shuddering. There was total silence in the graveyard, as if the whole world had come to a standstill.

Then, as if she had snapped out of a trance, Dervla began to rush about, picking up the banknotes. At the same time, Emma Delaney jumped over the wall, followed by Brendan and Molly. Dervla was so busy scrabbling for the money that she didn't see them until Emma was standing beside her.

"Dervla Gallagher, isn't it?" said Emma.

"No it's not," said Dervla sharply. "I'm Doctor Galvin, from California. And who are you?"

"Guard Emma Delaney," said Emma. "I'd like you to come to the station with me; we have one or two matters we'd like to clear up."

"You have the wrong person, Guard," said Dervla, trying to brazen it out. "And now if you'll excuse us, it's time we left." She went across to where Séamus lay on the ground, and said sharply, "Come on, we're leaving!"

Séamus only groaned, and began to sob.

"I would like both of you to come to the station," said Emma.

"We refuse," said Dervla. "We've done nothing." She continued to pull at Séamus, but he wouldn't get up. Finally she said furiously, "Dad! Dad! For God's sake, GET UP!"

Then she realised what she had said. She looked up at Emma, who was smiling triumphantly.

"So he is *your* father as well as Dervla's, Doctor Galvin," said Emma. "What a coincidence! Now let's go, shall we?"

Dervla was looking up at her like a hunted animal who has been cornered. Then she suddenly shouted, "NO! NEVER!" and got to her feet. Emma reached out to grab her, but Dervla dodged out of her grasp and, clutching the brief-case in her hand, she set off across the graveyard at surprising speed.

Emma raced after her, and so did the others. But Dervla was getting well ahead of them. Then Dessy pulled out all his running skills and sprinted after her, tearing like an Olympic athlete through the long grass.

Dervla was nearly at the gate when he caught up with her, made a flying tackle and caught her ankles. With a curse she stumbled and fell. Then she stood up and pushed Dessy away with her foot. As he fell back, he grabbed hold of the brief-case and held on to it.

"Give me that! Give me that, you little worm!" she shrieked, tugging at the brief-case. But Dessy held on. Seeing the others nearly upon her, Dervla decided to save herself, and made a final dash out of the gate. She climbed into the Land-Rover and it roared away down the road.

"She won't get far," said Emma, taking out her mobile phone. She phoned the Garda station and gave them the number of the Land-Rover. She told them about Dervla Gallagher and said she was bringing Séamus in.

With Locky's help, she got Séamus to his feet. He was still burbling with fear. "Don't let Sailor Jack at me, keep him away!" he moaned, as they frog-marched him across the graveyard.

As Billy's mother walked behind them with Molly and Brendan, she said, "What did you think of my performance?"

"It was superb, Mrs Bantam," said Molly, "just stupendous! Billy would have been so proud of you. What a pity the cameras weren't here to film it all."

"One camera is here, anyway," said Brendan, and he took a picture of Mrs Bantam striking a pose, and then one of her pointing back at the graveyard of Sailor Jack.

"Goodbye, ancestor!" said Mrs Bantam dramatically. "It was fun knowing you."

They were startled to hear, seemingly floating all

around them in the air, the chortling laugh of Sailor Jack.

"He seems to approve!" said Molly jokingly, but her heart was beating fast, as she remembered the strange sounds before, and the shaking and shuddering of the grave.

Brendan was remembering them too. He thought about the code and wondered what Sailor Jack would do if they cracked it and came back to find the treasure. He recalled the sound of the voice saying *Num . . . Num . . .* So surely Sailor Jack's spirit must have meant them to find it? Surely . . . ?

Emma handcuffed Séamus and bundled him into the back seat of the car. Brendan and Dessy sat on either side of him, just to make sure he didn't try to get out. But he was too exhausted from fear to put up any resistance, and no doubt he was glad to be taken away from the place where he had been haunted by the ghastly spectre of Sailor Jack.

In one last piece of defiance, he snarled, "You won't ever catch Dervla, you know. She's far too clever for any of you. And there's nothing much you can prove against me, anyway."

"I wouldn't be so sure of that," said Brendan, who was holding the brief-case. He opened it and pulled out some papers. He glanced at them and said, "They're print-outs of all the stuff that was in her computer back home. Names, fake family trees, the lot."

"That sure looks like proof to me," said Dessy.

"It does indeed," said Emma.

Séamus said nothing. He knew now that he was beaten.

When they reached the Garda station in town, Emma took Séamus inside. Brendan and Dessy walked to the hotel to meet Locky and Molly and Mrs Bantam, who had gone back in Locky's car.

"We must telephone Billy right away," said his mother, "and tell him all the news."

They gathered in her room while she phoned California. Billy was delighted. "Wow!" he said, "I wish I didn't have to stay here in California for the filming. All the action is in Ballygandon!"

Then he talked to Molly, Brendan and Dessy.

Molly told him that his mother had given a brilliant performance in the part of Mrs Morgan. She saw Billy's mother smiling and glancing at herself in the mirror and patting her hair.

Brendan said they must warn the Darlys that Séamus had been exposed as a fraud, so that they wouldn't go ahead with their plans to buy the house and start the heritage centre with Séamus in charge. Billy said, "Brad and Grace Darly are coming over to our house for a swim this afternoon. I'll put them wise. Hey, it's just great to talk to you guys. The Ballygandon Private Eyes have done it again!"

Dessy came on the line and told Billy about his prowess in American football. Then he said, "Hey,

Billy, what flag did Sailor Jack's pet seagull fly on his ship?"

"You tell me, Dessy," said Billy.

"The Gull and Crossbones!"

Later they all sat on the hotel's garden terrace having a large celebration tea. While the others recalled every moment of their triumph and the strange events in the graveyard, Brendan sat with his head bent over a big note-pad. Sheets of paper covered in figures and letters were scattered on the table. He had been trying all kinds of combinations to try to crack the code.

Suddenly he said, "The alphabet! That's the answer!"

"What do you mean?" asked Molly.

"Numbers, that's what the voice kept saying. If we link the numbers to the alphabet, and count from A onwards, that could give us the answer."

Molly read out the sentence from the inscription: *"I was born on the 7th day of the 1st month of the year 1829, at 5 o'clock in the morning."* Then she said, "So the first number is seven."

"Yes," said Brendan. He counted on his fingers as he said, "A, B, C, D, E, F, G . . . G is the seventh letter. Now, the first month, that would mean the first letter, which is A."

"The next number is 1829," said Dessy. "There aren't that many letters in the alphabet, unless they taught me wrong at school."

They all puzzled about this. Brendan said, "Well, the last bit says *5 o'clock in the morning*. And the fifth letter of the alphabet is E. So we've got a word that begins GA and ends with an E."

"What about *gamble*?" smiled Locky. "I guess Sailor Jack would have been a gambler as well as his other vices."

"Or maybe it's *gable*," said Molly, "like the gable on a roof."

"Could be," said Brendan. "The clue must be in the number 1829. Suppose we add the digits up? Let's see . . . " He wrote down the numbers 1, 8, 2 and 9 and added them.

"Twenty," said all five of them together.

Brendan counted through the alphabet and said, "The twentieth letter is T. We've got it! Put T between the GA and the E, and what do you get?"

Again they all cried together: "GATE!"

Then Brendan said, "The treasure must be buried by the gate of the graveyard. We must get there straight away. Grandpa, could you take us in your car?"

"I seem to be spending my entire time in that graveyard these days," said Locky. But they could tell that he was excited too.

They parked the car and the four treasure-seekers tumbled out and ran to the gate. There were two stone posts on either side. The top half of one of them had fallen away, and the stones were scattered around.

"We'll never move those," said Locky.

"We'll have to dig in the ground beside them, to see if we can reach underneath," said Molly. She took the spade she had borrowed from her father's garden shed, and began to dig.

"I wish we had another spade," said Brendan.

"Maybe the grave-digger left one lying around," said Dessy.

Locky said, "I've got a tool-kit in the car. There's some levers and things for taking tyres off in that." He rummaged in the boot of his car and produced some metal levers.

Brendan and Dessy each took one, and began helping Molly by scrabbling at the earth around the bottom of the standing gatepost. It was a slow business, but gradually they had dug away a hollow in the earth nearly a foot deep. Brendan reached down and felt the stones below ground level.

"Hey, one of these is loose!" he said. He put the end of the lever in the gap between the loose stone and the next one, and wiggled it about. The stone came out an inch or so. He was able to grasp it and pull. It was stiff, but little by little he pulled it away.

Then he lay down and reached his hand into the hole. "There's quite a big space here," he said. "Maybe there's something hidden inside."

Just as he was feeling around in the hole, there was a creak and a crack. A stone crashed from inside the pillar down into the hole. It just missed Brendan's hand.

At that moment Molly cried, "Brendan, look out! The gatepost is tilting over!" Sure enough, the stone pillar, its base in the earth loosened, was gradually leaning to one side, right above where Brendan was lying. Soon it would fall and crush him.

"Grab him!" shouted Locky. He took hold of one of Brendan's feet, and Molly seized the other. Dessy took an arm, and all together they pulled Brendan sharply away. He rolled over out of the way, just as the stone gatepost crashed down on the spot where he had been.

They all looked in alarm at the tumbled stones as the dust settled, thinking how near Brendan had been to disaster. The fallen stones had left the hole Brendan had been groping in open to view. There was a pile of dead grass and straw in it.

Molly knelt down and pulled the covering away. There in the hole was a small metal chest, covered in brown rust and dirt.

They all gazed at it in wonder. "Sailor Jack's treasure!" said Molly.

"Let's open it," said Dessy.

They pushed the end of one of the levers against the edge of the lid. They tried it at the front, and then at the side. Finally, with two levers pushing at the same time, they loosened the lid, and Brendan raised it.

The chest was empty.

"I guess someone got here before us," said Locky.

Then Molly said, "Look, there's some writing scrawled on the inside of the lid." She peered closer and read out: *"Sorry, shipmates, I spent it! And all that was left has gone to the bottom. Sailor Jack."*

"Well, it looks as if Sailor Jack has had the last laugh," said Dessy.

"Gone to the bottom," said Molly. "Whatever's left is at the bottom of the ocean, we'll never find it now."

"Just a minute," said Brendan, feeling in the box. "I think the bottom of this box is loose. Maybe that's what he meant." Once more he took the lever and fiddled around with the metal on the floor of the box. Soon he prised up the flat metal plate, to reveal a shallow compartment underneath. There was something there, an object wrapped in a piece of black cloth.

Brendan took it out and held it in his hands. Molly unwrapped the cloth. There before them was a large gold necklace with a big medallion in the centre, shaped like a skull and crossbones. It was studded with diamonds and rubies. "The last of Sailor Jack's treasure," said Brendan, as they all leaned over to stare at it.

"I'm sure that's worth a fortune," said Dessy.

"And *I'm* sure it's mine!" They heard the harsh voice rasping out the words, just as a hand reached in over their heads and grabbed the necklace. They looked up, and saw Dervla Gallagher. Why had she come back to the graveyard? Then Molly remembered the bank-notes that had been scattered all around in the struggle.

"Give that back!" shouted Brendan, but Dervla had taken them by surprise, and was too quick for them. Clutching the necklace, she set off into the graveyard and began snatching up the notes with her other hand wherever she could find them, and stuffing them in the pocket of her jacket.

"Don't let her get away!" cried Dessy, setting off at a sprint across the graveyard, followed by Brendan and Molly. Seeing them approaching, Dervla decided it was time to run. But her pursuers were between her and the gate. She looked around in panic, then remembered the wall behind Sailor Jack's grave where she had seen her captors appear before.

There must be a way out through the woods there, she thought, and raced in that direction. Just as she passed Sailor Jack's grave, she gave a shriek and stumbled, falling to the ground.

"No, no! Let go of me!" she cried.

Her pursuers hadn't yet reached her, so Brendan wondered who she was talking to.

"Let go, let go!" she cried again, seeming to struggle to pull her foot away. Something unseen was holding fast to her ankle. A ghostly laugh echoed around the graveyard.

Just as the trio came up to her and held her down, there was a rustle in the bushes and over the wall came Emma Delaney and another Guard.

"We thought she might come back for the rest of the money," said Emma, "so we decided to stake out the graveyard."

The Guards came over and got Dervla up, then put handcuffs on her wrists.

She didn't resist. She just stood there sobbing, and staring down at Sailor Jack's grave. "His hand!" she moaned, "his hand came and grabbed me by the ankle. I couldn't get free."

Brendan, Molly and Dessy looked at each other. They had seen nothing, but they felt they knew very well whom Dervla had seen.

Emma took the necklace from Dervla, then said, "You can keep the money." Dervla looked surprised.

Molly grinned and said, "It's fake, it's just some money they use in the movies."

Dervla scowled and said, "You double-crossing little gits!"

"That will be another treasure for the National Museum," said Locky, "like the Ballygandon Hoard. We'll make sure they display it with the full story of the Ballygandon Gang who found it. What's more, they're bound to give you a reward for finding it."

The Guards led Dervla across the graveyard towards the gateway. The others followed. As Brendan, Molly and Dessy reached the gate, they stopped and looked back in the direction of Sailor Jack's grave.

146

"Listen!" said Molly. They seemed to hear Sailor Jack's laughter floating in the air all around them. It was no longer menacing, but triumphant and jovial. The laughter gradually grew fainter and fainter, then faded away altogether.

"Goodbye, Sailor Jack!" said Molly quietly. There was no sound in reply, only a brooding silence lying over Lisbeg and its mystery graves.

Published by Poolbeg

The Phantom Horseman

by

GORDON SNELL

There are mysteries lurking at Horseshoe House, as Brendan and Molly discover when their grandfather goes to live there. Together with their friend Dessy, they explore the grounds and find an ivy-covered monument, said to be haunted by the spectre of a Horseman who died trying to jump over it. A threat of doom hangs over the house until his lost horseshoe is found.

Soon the trio find that the threat looks like coming true as they unearth shady goings-on at the house. Determined to unmask the villains, they face many dangers including weird apparitions, a narrow escape at a race meeting, a kidnapping and a chase after hidden gold.

A chilling adventure for readers 8 – 12 years old in the tradition of Enid Blyton.

ISBN: 1-85371-797-5